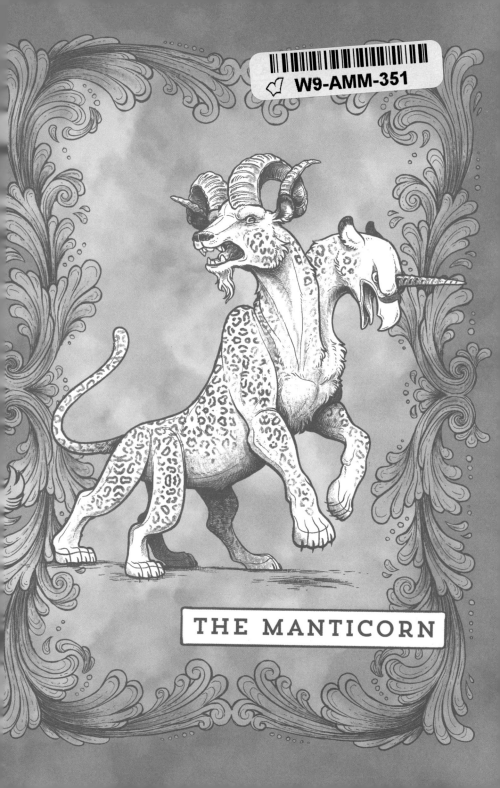

THE MANTICORN

LAIR OF THE BEAST

"A fast-paced, refreshingly creative adventure that will thrill readers from the very first page."

—Shannon Messenger, *New York Times*–bestselling author of the Keeper of the Lost Cities series and the Sky Fall series

"Fabulous characters and a unique mythology combine to create something really wonderful. *Snared* will ensnare you."

—Michael Scott, *New York Times*–bestselling author of The Secrets of the Immortal Nicholas Flamel series

"Pure dungeon-crawling fun. Witty and page-turning, I never knew what cheerful mayhem was waiting just around the bend. I can't recommend it enough."

—Zack Loran Clark, coauthor of *The Adventurers Guild*

"An imaginative blast of dungeon-crawling adventure with hilarious monsters and dastardly traps. Zany, heartfelt fun for everyone."

—Lou Anders, author of the Thrones & Bones series

"*Snared* is chock-full of quirky characters, fantastic world-building, and wild, hilarious adventure with every turn of the page. I loved it and kids will love it too!"

—Liesl Shurtliff, *New York Times*–bestselling author of *Rump*

"A thrilling fantasy adventure full of humor and heart. Adam Jay Epstein has created a fun, magical world readers will want to stay lost in."

—Jeff Garvin, author of *Symptoms of Being Human*

# SNARED

## LAIR OF THE BEAST

## ADAM JAY EPSTEIN

[Imprint]
MAKE YOUR MARK

New York

[Imprint]
MAKE YOUR MARK

A part of Macmillan Publishing Group, LLC
175 Fifth Avenue, New York, NY 10010

Library of Congress Cataloging-in-Publication Data is available.

ISBN 978-1-250-14695-3 (hardcover) / ISBN 978-1-250-14694-6 (ebook)

Our books may be purchased in bulk for promotional, educational, or business
use. Please contact your local bookseller or the Macmillan Corporate and
Premium Sales Department at (800) 221-7945 ext. 5442 or by email
at MacmillanSpecialMarkets@macmillan.com.

Book design by Eileen Savage

Imprint logo designed by Amanda Spielman

First edition, 2019

1  3  5  7  9  10  8  6  4  2

mackids.com

*Burglemeisters beware!*
*Steal this book, lose your hair*
*And grow moss instead*
*Upon your head!*

FOR ROSE AND LUCA

# TABLE OF CONTENTS

# MAZE OF THE DISSOLVED

At the end of a long torch-lit hall, four blinking eyes, each as big as a slither troll's fist, adorned a stone arch. They were restlessly shifting back and forth, scanning the area for intruders. Wily recognized the enchanted trap at once. There had been one just like it in Carrion Tomb, the dungeon in which he had spent his childhood.

"It's an Archway of Many Eyes," he explained to his companions, who were standing behind him in the shadowy entrance tunnel to the Maze of the Dissolved.

"I know what it is," Odette said, flicking a strand of blue hair from her face. "This isn't the first dungeon we've raided. More like the hundredth." The acrobatic elf gave Wily a big grin. It was still early in the morning, and she was always extra cheerful before lunch (even if they were deep inside a dangerous maze).

"Let's not exaggerate," Pryvyd, the one-armed Knight of the Golden Sun, said. "We've only explored eighty at the very most."

Righteous, Pryvyd's former arm, now disembodied and floating beside him, started moving its fingers as if counting in its head—not that Righteous actually had a head—or a body for that matter.

"Back me up here, Moshul," Odette said, turning to the giant moss golem.

Moshul, lacking a mouth, signed quickly to the knight with his big mud fingers.

"I'm not including the haunted temples or the swamp towers," Pryvyd countered.

Moshul signed back in response. Despite knowing Moshul for many months now, Wily was still struggling to learn sign language.

"That was a castle," Pryvyd said. "Not a dungeon."

Moshul signed again even more emphatically.

The knight relented. "Fine, if you include the temples *and* the towers *and* the castles, we might have raided a hundred."

Odette seemed very pleased with herself.

"I don't think the exact number of dungeons you've explored is important right now," Roveeka, Wily's adopted hobgoblet sister, interjected.

"She's right," Wily said. "Once those eyes spot us, an alarm will sound, and every creature in the maze will know we're here." He tapped his thumb against the wrist of his other hand. It was something he did when he was thinking hard, like when he was trying to solve a riddle or studying a complicated machine. Or coming up with a clever plan. "But that's only *if* the eyes spot us," he said with a sly grin.

He moved to Moshul's side and plucked a dark purple mushroom off his elbow. The moss golem was like a walking garden: vines, toadstools, and vegetables shared space on his lush green body with a hundred different kinds of crawling worms and insects. Wily handed the plump fungus to Roveeka.

"Roveeka," Wily asked, "how's your aim with mushrooms?"

"Almost as good as it is with knives," Roveeka said, weighing the mushroom in her hand.

During Roveeka's days in Carrion Tomb, she had served as a knife tosser, helping to ambush adventurers searching for treasure. Although she still carried her two precious knives, Mum and Pops, she had been practicing throwing other objects as well since escaping the dungeon with Wily.

"It needs to land just below the arch," Wily said. He turned to the others. "When it strikes the ground, move fast. Don't worry about being quiet. It's an Archway of Many Eyes, not ears."

Pryvyd and Righteous gave Wily matching bronze-plated thumbs-ups.

"Fast is not a problem for me," Odette said with a

grin. "The question is whether I'm going to do backflips as I sprint."

Roveeka cocked her hand and, with a flick of her lumpy wrist, flung the mushroom through the air. It hit the stone ground just below the archway and exploded into a cloud of thick black smoke.

"Now!" Wily urged the others.

Odette shot forward in a dazzling sequence of leaps and tumbles, quickly disappearing into the smoke ahead. Moshul grabbed Roveeka by the back of her shirt and tucked her under his arm as he took heavy lumbering steps toward the archway. With Righteous floating by his side, Pryvyd charged ahead, his bronze armor squeaking, clearly in need of a greasing.

Wily raced after his companions into the cloud of black. He could hear his companions moving on either side of him, but the smoke was so thick that he couldn't even see his own fingers. Worse still, with each breath, his nostrils were invaded by the pungent odor of rotting carrots. The purple mushroom had created an excellent smoke screen, but its smell left much to be desired.

After three dozen steps, Wily emerged from the smoke. With a loud gasp, he sucked in a lungful of cave air. His vision cleared, and he saw Odette already standing there, twiddling her fingers as if she had been waiting hours for his arrival.

Pryvyd, Moshul, and Roveeka stepped out of the haze just as it began to dissipate.

"Did the eyes spot us?" Pryvyd asked, "or did we get by unnoticed?"

"There's no way to tell out here," Wily answered. "The alarm doesn't sound in the main tunnels of the dungeon, only in the hidden maintenance tunnels. We'll just have to go deeper to find out."

The group continued down the long corridor to a room whose walls and ceiling were covered in snaking roots and dangling vines. In the middle of the room, a stout man with a tool belt stood on a ladder. He was busy sharpening a row of swinging blades and seemed completely unaware of their presence.

Wily knew at once that this man had to be the maze's trapsmith. Just a few months ago, before he learned that he was in fact the Prince of Panthasos, Wily had been just like him, stuck doing the mundane tasks that kept the dungeon operating smoothly. He had spent years sweeping Carrion Tomb's crypts, sharpening the spikes, feeding the rats, and greasing the gears of the crushing walls.

As the stout man performed his monotonous task, he sang an off-key tune:

"Got to keep the blades swinging, swinging, swinging overhead.

Got to keep the snakes biting, biting, make sure they're well fed.

Got to keep the slime dripping, dripping, then I'll go to bed."

Wily hadn't sung while he performed his duties, but now, thinking back, perhaps it would have made the endless stretches of dullness pass more quickly. Of course there was a lot Wily didn't know back then. He had been convinced by Stalag, the master of Carrion Tomb, and his surrogate father, that he was a hobgoblet rather than the human he actually was. And he had believed Stalag's other lies as well: that the sun would melt the skin clean off his bones the moment he left Carrion Tomb. And, worst of all, that his parents had been killed when in fact they were very much alive. His mother was the famous freedom fighter known as the Scarf and his father was the recently dethroned Infernal King. There were still mornings when Wily woke from slumber and didn't think any of it was true—just a wild, dizzying dream.

Wily spied the exit on the other side of the room. He signaled his friends to move for it. The trapsmith did not seem to have the slightest clue that Wily and his fellow adventurers were silently sneaking through the shadows along the perimeter of the room. As Wily and the others tiptoed out of the room of dangling roots, he heard the trapsmith begin a new song.

"*My sister kissed a troll down by the river.*
*She thought that kiss would break a cursed spell.*
*But that troll was just a troll down by the river.*
*Still, she married him and now they're doing well.*"

The group moved down a short hall and stopped before the entrance to a cavernous room strewn with skulls and bones. Peering inside, Wily could see a giant fanged bear sleeping soundly on the floor. A spine of sharp needles grew all the way down its back.

"A quill grizzler," Pryvyd said with a tremble of fear.

Although Wily had never seen one in the flesh before, he had heard stories of this fearsome creature. It was rumored to be capable of tearing a dragon in two with a single twist of its mighty fists. But, at this moment, it was extremely difficult to imagine this particular quill grizzler doing anything of the sort; it was snuggling a fluffy stuffed sheep while sucking on its own clawed thumb.

"Ohhh," Roveeka said, "he's so cute."

"Adorable," Odette added. "When he's not ripping your arms off."

"Shhh," Pryvyd said, "I'd rather not wake him."

Wily and his fellow adventurers walked silently through the cavern. As he moved past the snoring animal, Wily thought about how just yesterday he had been enjoying a plate of cookies in the palace garden with his mother, thinking his days of dungeon crawling might be over. Then adventure had called on him once more.

Since the defeat of the Infernal King, Pryvyd and the Knights of the Golden Sun had been desperately searching Panthasos for Stalag. If the rumors were true, the pale-skinned master of Carrion Tomb had been crisscrossing the land, meeting cavern mages, dungeon lords, and catacomb witches with a promise: if they joined his army and helped him overthrow the new prince—Wily—no longer would they have to hide away in their caverns, dungeons, and catacombs behind traps and foul beasts. They could keep their treasures in the grand castles of the Above. They could live in the sunlight without the fear of being driven away and having their loot stolen.

Despite Pryvyd's best efforts, Stalag always managed to stay ahead of them. Wily's mother had offered a reward to anyone who knew where Stalag would head next, but no one had come forward with anything helpful.

Then, yesterday, an old locksage smelling of dried squid had visited the palace with a valuable piece of information. The locksage told Wily and his mother that while he didn't know where Stalag was, he knew of something that could help them find him. He said that the Sludge Duke kept an enchanted compass hidden inside his Maze of the Dissolved. Unlike a normal compass, which always points north, this enchanted compass could point in the direction of anything that the holder wished to find as long as they had a small bit of metal to give the compass the magnetic scent, whether it be an incredible treasure, their true love, or the cruel surrogate father who had kept them trapped in a dungeon for the first twelve years of their life. The Sludge Duke had created the compass to find his lost Ring of Rodents, the only thing that made him happy, but when the compass led him to a bottomless pit, the furious duke buried it deep within the maze, promising misery for all who hoped to retrieve it.

The locksage said that getting to the compass would be very tricky and dangerous; it would take some very talented dungeon explorers to survive the maze. Fortunately, Wily and his companions were just that.

With the quill grizzler still nursing his clawed thumb, the group hurried out of the large room and down the next hall. Wily kept his eyes down, scanning the floor for pressure plates and traps. He was startled when a gruff voice called out from up ahead.

"What are you doing here?"

Wily looked up to see a boarcus leaning against the wall, holding a plate of salted crab. The hairy, tusk-faced guard stood tall with surprise.

"How'd you sneak past the Archway of Many Eyes without sounding the alarm?" the boarcus asked, the words slobbering through his large flabby lips.

"We didn't sneak past," Wily bluffed, while out of the corner of his eye, he could see Roveeka reach for Mum and Pops, tucked into her waistband. "That would be impossible. We're the new recruits."

There was a reason that boarcus were never used as the first or second or even third line of defense. They were extremely dim and thickskulled. Their primary purpose in a dungeon was to wander about and look intimidating.

"Hmmm," the boarcus said, thinking hard. "Then shouldn't you be in the Hall of Swords?"

"Yes," Wily said, feigning embarrassment. "We must have gotten lost. It is a maze, after all."

The boarcus considered this last statement for a long moment, then came to a conclusion. "That makes sense," he said, relaxing his overworked brain.

Roveeka let her hands fall from her knives.

"Here's my trick to keep from getting lost," the boarcus added with a curl of his snout. "You never walk around without a map. I got the Sludge Duke to draw one on the back of my shield. That's what I did."

The boarcus pulled the shield off his hairy arm and proudly showed them the inside. Etched into the metal was a very detailed map of the Maze of the Dissolved.

"What a brilliant idea," Odette said. "Maybe I can borrow yours."

"Hmmm," the boarcus considered. "If invaders come, I may need my shield to defend myself."

"As if any invader would get past the quill grizzler," Odette said with grin.

"You do have a point," the boarcus said. "But I don't know . . ."

"What if I offered to trade you my leftovers at dinner for it?"

With that, the boarcus handed the shield over to Odette with a smile big enough to lift his tusks.

"So where are we?" Pryvyd inquired, gesturing to the shield map.

"You really are confused," the boarcus said. "We're right here." He pointed to a spot near one of the shield's handles.

"And just to get my bearings," Wily asked, "where is the enchanted compass?"

"The treasure room is here." The boarcus moved his finger to a spot at the bottom of the shield, then pointed down the hall before them. "Which is that way. But you want to be heading in the other direction, back past the quill grizzler."

"And what did you draw down here?" Odette asked, pointing to a dot in the center of the shield map.

"I can't tell what you are pointing to," the boarcus said, squinting through the tufts of hair just below his eyes. He leaned in for a closer look.

As he put his tiny eyes up to the etched map, Odette smashed him in the face with the back of the shield. The boarcus collapsed to the floor.

"He'll just take a quick nap," Odette said with a glint of mischievousness in her eyes.

Wily and his companions took off fast, following the map on the back of the shield toward the treasure room. Moshul scooped Roveeka up and tucked her under his arm to make sure she didn't slow them down; Roveeka might have been an expert knife- and mushroom-thrower, but she wasn't a sprinter, and there was no time to waste. It would be only a matter of time before another guard found the unconscious boarcus lying on the floor and raised the alarm to alert everyone that there were intruders in the maze.

Despite the danger of traps and monsters, Wily was surprised to find he was overcome with a feeling of joy and freedom. Yes, life in the palace was wonderful, with its courtyards and banquets and grand libraries, but along with all the good came a tremendous amount of pressure. One day, not long from now, Wily would officially take the throne and become King of Panthasos. He would be responsible for the safety and well-being of everyone in the land. That would be an overwhelming task for even the most brilliant grown-up, let alone him, someone who only just last week had learned how to peel an orange. (One didn't find a lot of citrus fruits in a dungeon.) There was still so much that he needed to learn, including how to read, which was proving to be more of a challenge than he had expected. Wily didn't want to disappoint everybody. At times, the pressure to live up to expectations was suffocating him.

But here in a dungeon, in a world he knew like the back of his hand, with his friends by his side, all the worries of the Above seemed very far away.

# THE ENCHANTED COMPASS

Following the zigzagging lines on the shield map, the six companions sped through the twisting corridors at a breakneck pace. Wily traced his finger along the path. If the map was correct, the enchanted compass was just around the next bend.

"This way," Wily said as he shot off down the rightmost of three forking passages.

After one last turn, they found themselves at the edge of an underground lake. The lake was not filled with water, however, but thick green slime that bubbled and gurgled like slug stew over a crackling fire. At the center of the lake was a small island on which stood a stone pedestal. A rope bridge with wooden planks stretched from the room's entrance to the island.

"That must be the enchanted compass," Roveeka said excitedly as she looked across the lake.

Wily spied some kind of object resting atop the pedestal, but he couldn't make out its shape in the dim light. Once again he had to admire Roveeka's keen night vision.

Pryvyd was about to start for the bridge when Odette stopped him.

"Hold up," Odette said. "Rope bridges in dungeons and mazes have a tendency to collapse. Usually on purpose."

"Let me check," Wily said.

He walked up to the edge of the bridge and ran his finger along one of the rope's handrails. It was smooth on the top and rough on the bottom.

"Is it safe to cross?" Odette asked.

"It's very worn," Wily said. "And quite old."

"So it could snap at any moment?" Pryvyd asked, taking a step back.

"To the contrary," Wily countered. "The top of the rope has been smoothed by hundreds of hands holding it. It's not going anywhere. But that's also the bad news. It means whatever is lurking in that slime is the real danger."

"You made me feel better and worse all at once," Odette said.

"Most explorers walk slowly across a dangling bridge," Wily said. "They think it's safer. But if a slime squid is hidden below, being slow is the worst thing you could do."

Moshul shuddered at the mention of slime squid.

"I've got this," Wily continued. "I've been racing across hanging bridges my whole life."

Wily turned to Odette and plucked a metallic thread from her collar.

"What was that for?" Odette asked.

Instead of answering, Wily took a running start and sprinted across the gently swaying bridge. He had been told by the locksage that the enchanted compass needed a small bit of metal or stone to give it the magnetic scent of the object for which it would be searching. Odette was going to be his test subject. As he ran toward the island, he eyed the green ooze bubbling an arm's length below the bridge's wooden planks. He knew at any moment a long tentacle could burst forth, wrap around his ankle, and tug him into the slime. To his great surprise and relief, he made it to the island without being attacked.

Wily swiftly approached the pedestal and found a round object resting there that appeared to be molded from silver. It looked a lot like every other compass he had seen before. Yet when Wily picked up the object and inspected it, he found that there were a few distinct differences. The compass arrow was fixed in place so it couldn't spin or change direction. It also had a dozen holes around its outer perimeter that revealed that it was hollow inside. He wondered if this was, in fact, the enchanted compass and how it could possibly operate without a spinning arrow. Wily knew there was only one way to find out. He would test it.

*Find my friend Odette*, Wily thought as he rubbed the metallic thread from her tunic on the compass.

Wily stood and waited. Nothing happened. Perhaps this was not the compass after all. Disappointed, he took a step back toward the rope bridge. At once, the silver object in his hand began to whistle. When he stopped moving, it stopped making a sound.

He took another step toward the bridge. The object whistled again. Wily understood: the enchanted compass would whistle when he moved in the direction of the object he was seeking.

But before he could tell his friends what he had discovered, he heard Pryvyd scream, "Wily! It's time to leave! Now!"

Wily looked up to see faceless humanoids emerging from the slime around the small island on which he was standing. Their bodies and outstretched arms dripped with viscous green ooze. One of the strange creatures lunged at Wily. Instinctively, he blocked the attack with the boarcus's shield. In an instant, a hole formed in the center of the shield where the creature's slimy fingers made contact. Wily dropped the shield as the acidic green ooze ate its way through the metal. Within seconds, there was nothing left of the shield other than its leather straps.

Wily sprinted onto the rope bridge, and immediately the faceless humanoids changed course, dove back into the lake, and moved at a frightening speed through the slime. Before Wily had even made it halfway across the bridge, the figures started emerging near Pryvyd and Moshul.

Roveeka pulled out Mum and Pops, prepared to throw them at the attackers.

"Don't bother," Pryvyd shouted. "These must be the Dissolved. Legend says they can melt metal with a single touch."

"And rock and bone," Odette added, "and most other things, too."

When Wily finally reached the end of the bridge, he just kept moving, racing for the door out. Moshul scooped up Roveeka as Odette ran alongside Wily. Pryvyd had to grab Righteous, who was ready to do battle with the Dissolved, and drag it along.

"I don't care how brave you are," Pryvyd said to his arm. "You may not be attached to me, but you're still my arm."

The group sprinted out of the room, but the Dissolved were not ready to give up the chase. They followed Wily and the others into the maze of tunnels.

Odette looked back over her shoulder with concern. "If we hit just one dead end and are forced to backtrack," she said grimly, "the Dissolved will catch up to us. Even Moshul wouldn't stand a chance against them."

No sooner did Odette say that when they reached a crossing where the tunnel forked in three directions.

"Which way did we come from originally?" Pryvyd asked, looking at each tunnel in turn, clearly confused.

"I don't remember," Odette said, eyeing the three paths. "I was following Wily."

"We can use the map again," Roveeka said.

"It was on the shield," Wily informed her, "which is now a puddle of slime."

Looking back down the tunnel, Wily could see the Dissolved shambling toward them with their arms outstretched.

"We'll just have to take our chances," Odette said, moving toward the center tunnel.

Then, suddenly, Wily remembered what he was holding in his hand. "We've got something better than a map," he said, a glimmer of hope in his eye.

Wily bent over and plucked an iron pebble from the tread of his shoe he had picked up on their journey from the palace to the maze. Then he held the enchanted compass aloft in front of him.

"Compass, show us the fastest way out of here."

Wily stepped toward the center path, but the compass was silent. Then, he moved toward the tunnel to the left. The compass began to whistle loudly, so loudly, in fact, that Roveeka put a finger in her ear.

"It's certainly not a compass to use when you plan on sneaking," she said as they took off down the left path.

Wily was barely looking where he was going; instead he was letting the compass lead the way. Right. Left. Straight. Left again.

"The Dissolved are still on our tails," Pryvyd said. "Hurry!"

They ran past the boarcus, who was still slumped on

the ground. The clatter of feet woke the tusk-faced guard with a start.

"What's going on?" the confused boarcus blurted at the passing adventurers. "Are we being invaded?"

"Nope," Odette said. "All good. Just doing a little practice drill."

"You're very convincing," the boarcus said. "I really believed the panic on your faces."

The compass took them right back into the large cavern with the quill grizzler. Only this time, it was very angry and very awake. The creature stood menacingly in front of the room's only other exit, scratching its claws against the stone ground.

*This is bad,* Wily thought to himself. *Very, very bad.*

"Instead of asking the compass for the *fastest* way out," Odette said, "maybe you should have asked for the *safest* way out."

A booming growl bellowed from the quill grizzler's eight-foot-wide mouth.

"I know you can speak a lot of monster languages," Odette said to Wily. "Any chance you know what he just said?"

Wily shook his head. "We didn't have a quill grizzler in Carrion Tomb. And for good reason. They're known for feeding on their feeders."

Just then, the slime-dripping Dissolved entered the cave. They were about to shamble toward Wily and his companions when they spied the giant bear. The Dissolved quickly turned and fled.

"When even the mindless slime monsters run away," Odette said, "you know you're in trouble."

Pryvyd readied his spiked shield for battle. Roveeka pulled out Mum and Pops. Moshul stepped up beside Righteous, who was already swinging its sword.

But before anyone attacked, Odette started running toward a sunken portion of the cavern floor. She did a double backflip before grabbing something off the ground.

"Hey there, you big prickle puss!" Odette yelled. "I think you might want this."

She held aloft the stuffed sheep the quill grizzler had been snuggling before. After swinging it in two circles overhead, she tossed the sheep into a distant corner of the cavern.

The quill grizzler's eyes went wide with terror. It chased after its toy with a soft whimper, leaving the far exit of the chamber clear. The distraction had worked.

Everybody sprinted for the door. Unfortunately, as soon as they moved, the compass began to whistle loudly again. It snapped the quill grizzler back to attention. The giant beast changed direction and came lumbering after them. The mighty creature arched its back and shot a series of sharp needles at the fleeing adventurers. Pryvyd was able to deflect some with his spiked shield, and Righteous batted the others away with its sword.

Wily had nearly made it to the exit of the cavern when he felt the quill grizzler's claws snap closed around him. The fanged bear lifted him off his feet and began to squeeze. The pressure was intense, much more intense, Wily thought wistfully, than the pressure he had been feeling over the last few months in the palace.

Before Wily's world went dark, Righteous came flying up to the quill grizzler's face and grabbed a fistful of its nose hair. The hovering arm gave a hard tug. With a mighty yelp, the needle-backed bear released Wily, allowing him to run.

Wily sprinted through the cave exit just as the quill grizzler slammed against the too-small-to-fit-through door. As the monster tried to squeeze his head in between, Wily and the others took off together.

They continued through the room of swinging axes, where the trapsmith had been working earlier, ducking their heads to avoid the sharpened blades. They sprinted past the Archway of Many Eyes, not caring whether they were spotted, heading straight for the maze's exit and the circle of blue sky beyond it.

As they burst outside, Wily laughed with relief. They had retrieved the Enchanted Compass and survived the Maze of the Dissolved. The thrill of accomplishment gave him goose bumps all the way down his arms. Beaming with pride, he looked up at the cliffs that surrounded the maze's entrance. With a sense of calm, he took in the autumn yellow leaves that carpeted the mountainsides.

Roveeka sat down on a large hard rock and removed her sandals to massage her feet. "That was a close one," she said. "I think I need a pair of faster running sandals."

"What do you need running sandals for?" Odette asked. "Moshul was carrying you the whole time."

"Maybe he wouldn't have to," Roveeka responded, "if I had faster sandals."

Just then, from behind a bush, a seven-year-old boy and girl emerged. They had frightened looks in their eyes.

"Are you Wily Snare?" the boy asked. "The new Prince of Panthasos?"

Wily nodded with a puzzled look.

"How'd you know I was here?" he asked.

"We asked a passing merchant for help," the boy said. "He told us you had come this way."

"We saw you enter the maze from up the mountain," the girl said. "We tried to shout to you but you didn't hear us. So we just waited here, hoping you'd come out safely."

"Our town is in big trouble," the boy said. "We need your help at once."

The moment of relief and joy Wily had experienced blew away like a yellow autumn leaf in the mountain breeze. It felt as if the quill grizzler's claws were tightening around him once more. Wily was quite good at escaping from trap-filled dungeons, but escaping the pressures of being the Prince of Panthasos was turning out to be much more difficult.

# FROM BETWEEN TWO ROCKS

Despite the direness of their situation, the boy and the girl appeared to have just left a very formal party; both of them were dressed in green buttoned shirts and matching green shorts. Their hair was neatly brushed and combed. Even their fingernails were clean. The only thing slightly out of place was the faint odor of rotting tunnel trout clinging to them. It smelled as if they had been hiding in a fish barrel.

"It's just up thish mountain," the little boy said, pushing his blond hair out of his face.

"Yes," the girl quickly added. "Just up the mountain."

The boy scrambled up the rocky slope, taking big clumsy steps.

The girl beckoned the others to follow. "Hurry," she said. "Our family and neighbors are in grave danger."

"What's happened to your village?" Roveeka asked.

"It was the middle of our birthday party," the boy responded. "Everything was candy and cake, when out of nowhere came this big turtle dragon. Tearing up the whole town. Breaking things and all."

"A turtle dragon?" Odette asked with a puzzled look. "This far from the Chamango River? That's unusual."

"Perhaps it was a different kind of dragon," the young girl said, "but it definitely was big!"

"That's right," the boy chimed in as he hustled over a nest of brambles. "I was too busy being a scared little boy to know exactly what kind of dragon it was."

Wily raised an eyebrow at the strange response.

"Did it have long green antennae?" Pryvyd asked.

"Sheesh," the boy said, "you're asking an awful lot of questions. We just want you to save our village from the dragon. Not write a book about it."

Roveeka sidled up to Wily. "He's very rude," she said under her breath.

"There's no time for talking," the girl said, looking back over her shoulder. "You must save your energy for fighting the dragon, whatever kind it is."

"And she's not much better," Roveeka added.

"Something is off about them," Wily said quietly. "I don't think they're what they appear to be."

"Quit jibber jabbering," the boy called back. "Before I get all killy and the like on yoosh."

The girl slapped the boy in the shoulder hard.

He quickly changed his tone to light and sweet. "I mean, could you please stop talking and focus on walking, sir."

Wily felt a chill run up his spine. He knew someone else who had used words like *killy* and *yoosh*, and it wasn't a little boy with dirty blond hair and green knickers. Wily signaled Pryvyd, Odette, Moshul, and Righteous to come over to his side.

"Even the ghost spiders who eat their own mothers have better manners than those children," Roveeka whispered to her companions.

"They're not children," Wily said to the others. "It's Agorop and Sceely, Stalag's oglodyte minions. A powerful illusion must have been cast on them to change their appearance and even the sound of their voices."

Odette's blue eyes went to where the two children were bouncing up the hill in their matching outfits. She snapped her fingers as if figuring something out. "But an illusion can't change their smell," she sputtered. "They stink of old fish rotting on a cave floor. I should have realized it the moment they stumbled out of the bushes."

Pryvyd, Moshul, and Roveeka nodded in agreement.

"I knew there was something I didn't like about them," Roveeka said.

"I have a feeling," Wily said quietly, "that they're leading us right into a trap."

Pryvyd cleared his throat and called out to Moshul, who was a few steps ahead of them. The moss golem turned his jeweled eyes toward Pryvyd, and the knight quickly began to sign. Wily wasn't sure exactly what he was saying, but he had a pretty good idea.

The little boy, who Wily suspected was actually Agorop, looked over his shoulder to see what was slowing the group down.

"Please, kind heroes," the little boy said, "there's no time to waste. We must get to the town before our human families are swallowed up by the beetle dragon."

"He means 'turtle dragon,'" the little girl, who Wily guessed was Sceely, corrected quickly. "We are very sad and worried. We don't know what we're saying."

Suddenly, Moshul made a move for the two children with his big mossy hands extended.

"Whash you doing?" the little boy screamed with panic in his eyes.

"Get away, you pile of mud!" the little girl howled.

The two took off, scrambling to avoid the golem's fingers. The boy tripped on a rock, but before he hit the ground, Moshul scooped him up into his right hand. The little girl was moving faster, making a break for a cluster of high shrubs, but Righteous came flying up and grabbed her by the shoulder, slowing her down.

"Get your metal mitt off me," the young girl said, swatting at the floating arm.

She tried to break free, but Righteous had given Moshul enough time to catch up. The moss golem snagged her in his other hand. Both of the "children" struggled to free themselves.

"You can stop pretending," Wily told the captives when he reached Moshul's side. "We know who you are."

"Yoosh talking crazy and the like," the boy said. "I'm just a little boy. I isn't an oglodyte."

"Watch what you're saying," the girl yelled to the boy.

"Tell us what sort of trap you were leading us into," Pryvyd said.

"We're not ass-sist-erating you in any way," the boy said.

Moshul shook them both like a pair of baby rattles. As he did, the illusions faded away, exposing them as the slimy oglodytes they actually were.

"Okay! Okay!" Agorop yelled. "We'll lead ya to Stalag. We'll do whatever you want. Just make the mud man stop shaking me."

"Where is he?" Wily said.

"Just up the hill," Agorop stammered.

"How many soldiers does he have with him?" Pryvyd asked.

"He's alone," Sceely shouted down.

Roveeka looked up at Sceely skeptically.

"I don't believe her," Roveeka said. "Her eyes dart back and forth when she's lying."

"I'm telling the truth," Sceely said as her pupils danced.

Odette signed to Moshul, who began to shake them again.

"Stop! Stop!" Sceely screamed. "He's with two others. I swear."

Wily noticed that her eyes were no longer darting around. He turned to his fellow companions. "If it is just Stalag and two others against the six of us," he said with a burst of confidence, "we should be able to capture them. They've lost their most powerful weapon: the element of surprise."

With Agorop and Sceely still clutched tightly in Moshul's hands, the group continued up the mountain, following the now somber oglodytes' directions. Wily and his companions were led through a forest of dense trees and past patches of shoulder-high bamboo.

"Over there." Agorop gestured to a pair of giant boulders. "Stalag's just past those rocks."

Before the group could take another step, an ominous, hissing voice that Wily was all too familiar with announced, "You are just as small and pathetic as the day you left the tomb."

Wily turned to see Stalag step out from between the giant boulders with his hands raised over his head. The cavern mage's time in the Above hadn't made him any less frail; his bony arms still resembled the branches of a dying tree. His ghostly eyeballs swung loosely in the dark sockets above his cheeks. But Wily knew that in spite of Stalag's appearance, immense power resided inside the mage.

"Be a good son and hand over the enchanted compass," Stalag said, his words slithering from his cracked gray lips like vipers.

"Haven't you learned your lesson?" Odette said. "We've already defeated you twice. What makes you think that the third time will be any different?"

"Maybe the fact that I've come with more than just oglodytes and scorpions today?" Stalag said with a sneer of delight.

The boulders from which Stalag had emerged began to move. Or rather, stand up: the two rocks were not rocks at all but crouching stone golems. Unlike Moshul, these golems had features so lifelike and detailed that, had they been painted one of the many colors of human skin, they would appear to have been made of flesh and bone. One of the two had an alabaster beard, and the other had quartz fingers that sparkled in the sunlight.

The mighty stone golems, both triple the height of Moshul, marched toward Wily and his companions. With each of their steps, the earth shook with such force that it seemed as if the mountain itself might crumble in fear. Desperately, Wily looked around, trying to find a way to escape, but there was no cover or place to duck and hide.

"I told you there were only two others," Sceely cackled. "I just didn't tell you how big they are."

As the two stone golems got closer, Wily could see that they were both smiling.

The stone golem with the beard stopped before Moshul and looked down at him. Then he laughed a horrible laugh, and the ground around him started to shake.

"Where's your mouth, little brother?" His voice echoed like a wolf's howl in a canyon. "You lose it in the woods?"

"Or are you just too stupid to talk?" the quartz-fingered golem added with a booming chortle.

Moshul was furious. Thorns sprouted from the vines that curled all the way down his chest. He tossed the oglodytes in his hands to the ground.

"What are you going to do?" the bearded golem mocked him. "Throw a mud pie?"

"Or get some ants to crawl on us?" the quartz-fingered golem said with scorn.

"You're a mistake," the bearded golem taunted. "One that should have been squashed a long time ago."

With his mossy fingers squeezed tight, Moshul charged at the bearded golem.

*Thwap.*

The bearded stone golem swung his arm. The back of his hand struck Moshul in the chest. Wily watched as the moss golem was knocked to the ground as easily as a straw man.

Moshul pulled himself back to his feet while Odette and Pryvyd came running to his side. Pryvyd held his spiked shield aloft as Odette grabbed a broken bamboo shoot off the ground and spun it like a fighting stick.

"We stand together," Odette called out to the stone golems.

"Then you will fall together," the quartz-fingered golem said.

"And there's nothing you can do about it, silent one," the bearded golem added.

The bearded golem reached out and grabbed Moshul by the shoulders. He lifted him into the air and threw him—off the side of the mountain.

It happened so fast, Wily barely had a chance to realize what had occurred. Then Stalag began to laugh. It snapped Wily out of his stupor. He ran to the edge of the mountain and looked down. There, hundreds of feet below, Moshul lay on the ground, motionless.

When Wily turned back to the golems, he saw Pryvyd and Odette, both rage-filled, charging them. The quartz-fingered golem punched Pryvyd's shield so hard that every metal spike that had been sticking out from it was snapped clean off. Pryvyd tumbled backward, his brass armor clattering and clanging. Odette used her bamboo shoot to vault herself up onto the shoulder of the bearded golem. She tried to jab him in the neck with the makeshift fighting stick, but it snapped against his hard skin. The golem plucked her off his shoulder and viciously tossed her to the ground.

"I knew you'd be able to get me the compass," Stalag said, his frail hand outstretched. "Why do you think I told you right where it was?"

Wily remembered the locksage who had come to the palace the previous day and told him and his mother of the whereabouts of the compass. Had he been working for Stalag?

"Hand over the compass," Stalag said. "And the throne, for that matter. You're not fit to be king. Not now. Not ever. You're meant to have a trapsmith belt around your waist, not a crown on your head."

Wily was caught off guard. For all the lies Stalag had told, this time he was speaking a truth, a truth that Wily had not yet even fully admitted to himself: he wasn't ready to lead anyone, much less a whole kingdom. All he wanted to do now was get away before another one of his friends was hurt or thrown off a cliff.

Wily's mind worked at breakneck speed. He knew they couldn't defeat these golems in a fight, and running away wasn't an option either; for every twenty stops he and his friends took, the golems would need only one. No, they needed another way to escape.

"Give me the compass!" Stalag demanded once more.

*I need to invent something,* Wily thought. *But what could I make in mere seconds? Not a flying machine or a speedy boat.*

Wily scanned the hillside for anything at all. Then his eyes fell on Pryvyd. And his shield.

Wily pulled out the compass and handed it to Roveeka.

"Throw this over the golems' heads, as far as you can," Wily said, gesturing to the golems.

"But we came all this way for it," Roveeka said.

"It won't do us any good if we're prisoners," Wily said as the stone golems moved in on them. "And even less if we're dead."

Roveeka nodded and tossed the compass as hard as she could. It flew up and over the golems' heads.

Stalag's ghostly eyes shook in their sockets as he watched the magical device take flight. "Don't let the compass break," he hissed to the golems. "Catch it!"

Both of the stone golems turned for the flying compass and went chasing after it.

Wily seized the moment and ran for Pryvyd.

"Your shield!" Wily said. "Give it to me, quick."

"But the spikes have been broken off."

"That's why I need it."

Pryvyd tossed it to him.

Wily reached into his tool belt and pulled out a vial of slither troll slime. He slathered the smooth outside surface of the shield with the slippery goo. Then, he lay the shield down on the side of the hill while keeping a firm grip on its edges to hold it in place.

"Everybody on!" Wily shouted to the others.

Roveeka and Odette jumped aboard the curved shield. Pryvyd plucked Righteous out of the air and squeezed onto the shield as well. Wily jumped on last, releasing his grip, and immediately the shield took off down the hill like a sled.

"Don't let them escape!" Stalag screamed to Agorop and Sceely. The two oglodytes raced after the companions, but their webbed feet couldn't keep pace with the ever-increasing speed of the shield.

Wily was about to give a shout of relief when Roveeka pointed to a sea of trees ahead. "That's not good."

"How do you steer this thing?" Odette shouted to Wily, who was right behind her.

"We've got to use our weight," Wily said.

He could see that they were heading straight for a very large oak tree.

"Lean to the right!" Wily shouted.

All four of them shifted their weight to the right. Even Righteous tilted in the same direction. The shield and everyone on it nearly tipped over. Wily's elbow scratched against the pebbly ground. But they made it past the tree, if only by a hand's length.

"If we had hit that—" Odette began to say before Pryvyd cut her off.

"Another tree!" he shouted.

Now the out-of-control shield sled was heading straight for a twisted pine.

"Lean left!" Wily shouted.

Everybody shifted their weight again. They missed, but the tip of the shield scraped the bark off the base of the pine tree, leaving a thick gash in the wood and sticky sap all over the shield.

Far behind them, Wily could still hear Stalag screaming. "Don't let them get away!"

"Weeze can't keep up," Agorop shouted back.

The shield sled snaked through a cluster of dense trees and finally bounded out onto the open mountainside. Wily turned around and was relieved to see that Stalag and the oglodytes were no longer visible in the distance.

"Hey, brilliant inventor," Odette asked. "How do we stop this thing?"

This was a very good question that Wily didn't have an immediate answer to. "It will slow down on its own once we get to the bottom," he said weakly.

"We may be getting to the bottom faster than you expected," Odette said.

Wily looked ahead and saw that the sled was racing straight for the edge of a massive cliff. There was no way to turn left or right—both would lead to the same steep drop.

"We have to jump off!" Pryvyd shouted.

"No!" Wily yelled. "We're moving too fast. We'll roll right off the edge. We need to slow the shield."

Wily snatched Righteous's sword from its hand. He jabbed the tip of the blade into the ground behind them.

The metal prong dug into the earth, leaving a trail of dirt behind, but it wasn't enough to slow down the shield.

"Use anything you got," Wily yelled.

The edge of the cliff was rapidly approaching. Roveeka pulled Mum and Pops from her waistband and jabbed the knives into the ground on either side of the shield. Still, it wasn't enough.

Odette pulled a coil of rope out from her shoulder satchel and tied a slipknot at one end.

"Righteous, loop this around that tree branch!" Odette said, pointing to a lone tree on the edge of the cliff.

Pryvyd grabbed his floating arm and threw it like a spear. Righteous flew straight for the tree and quickly tied Odette's rope around it.

"Everyone hold on to the rope," Odette screamed.

Wily wrapped his fingers around it tightly as he watched the cliff's edge get closer and closer and closer—

And then the shield went airborne, and Wily and his companions soared out over the chasm. His fingers clutching the rope, Wily began to fall.

Two seconds later, he felt himself lurch backward as the rope went taut. The shield slipped out from under him as he tightened his grip. Wily and the others went swinging back toward the cliff face, smacking into it hard.

Looking down, Wily saw the shield fall. After a few seconds, it hit the floor of the rocky canyon with a loud *clang.* Although he wasn't in the most ideal position right now, he was far better off than where he could have been.

A hand reached down from above. It was Righteous. The hovering arm helped pull Wily, Roveeka, Odette, and Pryvyd to safety. Once everybody was back on the mountain slope, the group took a moment to collect themselves.

"I can't believe we lost Moshul," Odette said, and Wily saw a single tear roll down her cheek.

"You know what he would have told us," Pryvyd said. He moved his left hand away from his chest and stretched his fingers out, wiggling them slightly. "Onward into the light," Pryvyd said aloud, "He would want us to go on. He would want us to catch Stalag and make sure he won't be a danger to Panthasos any longer."

Wily was barely listening. He was furious with himself. *I'm a trapsmith. I should have known better. I should have realized that we were walking right into a trap. If I had been a little more cautious, a little more careful, Moshul might still be standing over us right now.*

A friend had been lost, and it was all his fault.

# 4

## A SAD WALK HOME

Wily had hoped to return to the royal palace of Panthasos with his head held high, clutching the enchanted compass in hand. Instead, he and his companions were coming back far worse than when they had started: the compass was gone, Stalag had it, and Moshul was dead.

With every step that Wily took, it seemed as if he were pulling himself through a thick swamp of giant-slug slime.

"Have I told you about the time Moshul and I went to the Raven's Nest?" Odette asked.

Instead of grieving silently, elves told stories about the loved ones they had lost. For thirty days after their passing, friends and family would share tales of the dead to keep their spirit and memory alive. Odette had been recounting her adventures with Moshul for the last eight hours.

"I don't think so," Wily said with a heavy heart.

"I'd like to hear about it," Roveeka said, trying to brighten the mood.

Ever since Wily had met Roveeka in Carrion Tomb as a toddler, she had been able to see the light in the darkest tunnel. It was one of the many reasons why Wily was so glad to have chosen her to be his surrogate sister.

"The Raven's Nest is the secret gathering spot of the sneakiest burglemeisters in all of Panthasos," Odette explained. "What makes the gathering spot so secret is that it's on the third floor of a building with no stairs leading up to it. The Burglemeister Society believes that a true thief should be able to climb up the outside of the building and sneak through a window. Now, being a skilled acrobat, the task posed no challenge for me. Moshul, on the other hand, has a lot of talents, but climbing isn't one of them."

"*Had* a lot of talents," Wily corrected her sadly.

"Right," Odette nodded grimly. "Had. Thank you for the unnecessary reminder, Wily."

She pushed on with her story. "But Moshul wasn't going to just let me go into a den of thieves and criminals alone. He wanted to be by my side. So, what'd he do? He built his own staircase. He took the stones from a nearby wall and started stacking them on top of each other. When he came crashing through the window of the Raven's Nest, the entire place went silent. No one knew what to do. They were too scared to accuse him of cheating his way in, so instead they started buying him drinks. Which is extra funny because he has no mouth."

"*Had* no mouth," Wily corrected her again.

"Right," Odette added. "Had." Her shoulders slumped as she became lost in thought.

As the group came around Trumpet Pass, Wily caught sight of the royal palace, with its high marble walls and newly planted orchard. He remembered the first time he had seen the palace or, as it had been known then, the Infernal Fortress. Just a few months ago, the walls that were now as white as an albino eel had been stained black with dripping tar. Spinning blades had moved along hidden tracks in the stone to keep intruders away. The palace that his father, the Infernal King, had ruled over was a desolate place filled with traps and monsters of the most unfriendly variety. Wily had changed all that: the traps had been removed and replaced with libraries and sitting rooms. The only monsters left in the palace were a shy giant slug he had rescued from Carrion Tomb and the Skull of Many Riddles who, not needing to set rooms ablaze anymore, had become the palace's court jester, telling riddles to amuse and entertain.

As the weary companions approached the palace, Wily could see that the drawbridge was down, stretching across the moat. He had decided shortly after taking residence in the palace that the drawbridge should remain down and the gate open at all times. Pryvyd had warned him that it was unsafe, especially with Stalag still on the loose, but Wily had insisted. He wanted his new home to bear no resemblance to the one he had lived in for the first fourteen years of his life. In Carrion Tomb, everything was built to keep people out and away. Here, he wanted to welcome people in.

On either side of the palace gate, a Knight of the Golden Sun stood guard. They both wore the same bronze armor as Pryvyd, and each held a shield decorated with their order's symbol: a shining orb with eight golden arms reaching out from it.

"Welcome back," one of the soldiers called out cheerfully, her silver face paint sparkling in the daylight.

Wily didn't have the strength or will to say anything. He just wanted to eat, hug his mom, and go to bed. It didn't even matter that it was many hours before the sun would set.

Wily and the others passed the guards silently on their way into the palace atrium, which was decorated with objects from all over Panthasos. When Wily was officially anointed prince, people from across the land had brought many gifts in celebration. Wily had decided to place them here, in the atrium, so that every visitor to the palace could share in their beauty. There were eagle feathers from the high mountain elves, a blood ruby that pulsed with color as if it had a beating heart inside, and a wreath of petrified flowers grown in the rock gardens of the desert basin. There was even an unbreakable metal crown forged in the legendary eversteel furnace of Drakesmith Island, gifted to Wily by the seafaring Brine Baron.

Continuing through the atrium, the group passed under a large flag that hung from the ceiling. Unlike the flag of his father, which was decorated with a frightening three-horned helmet, Wily's palace banner signaled a new era when machines would not be built to destroy or control; it depicted a metal gear interlocked with the branches of a tree. Wily had dreamed up the image himself and thought it conveyed the mission he'd set for himself: to ensure that human inventions worked in tandem with nature to make Panthasos more prosperous for all. But right now, Wily couldn't imagine how he'd ever achieve anything of note. He left the atrium without even glancing up at the flag.

Wily led Roveeka, Odette, Pryvyd, and Righteous down the long hallway to the grand sitting room. Inside, Wily spied his mother, Lumina Arbus, staring down at a large map of Panthasos unfurled on the oak table. Although she no longer wore a rainbow of colored scarves over her face like when she was a noble bandit fighting the tyranny of the Infernal King, she still kept a pendant of rainbow colors around her neck as a reminder of who she used to be. On the table beside the map, Lumina's two pet ferrets, Gremlin and Impish, wrestled over a quill pen. They poked at each other with their paws while Wily's mother eyed the map.

"Would you two cut it out?" Lumina said in a huff. "If you each want a quill pen, there are plenty more in the upstairs study."

That was not a good enough answer for either Gremlin or Impish, who seemed to only want the one they were currently fighting over.

Pryvyd, Roveeka, Odette, and Righteous waited just outside the hall as Wily stepped in. "Hi, Mom," Wily said with no life in his voice.

Lumina looked up, and her expression immediately transformed from frustration to joy. "Wily!" his mother said. "You're back safe."

Lumina moved swiftly toward her son. Impish and Gremlin both dropped the quill pen and excitedly followed. Wily felt his mother's arms wrap tightly around his body as he slumped into her. He pressed his head against her shoulder and she kissed his temple.

The hug was as warm and comforting as a bowl of chicken soup. No matter how many times he embraced his mother, it still had this incredible power. He wondered if there was some kind of special magic that caused a hug to feel so good. Once he finally learned to read, he would have to check the library's spell books to find out.

"Can I get you something to eat?" Lumina asked as

she pulled back to get a good look at her long-lost son. "A sandwich? Or a bowl of fruit?"

"I really don't have much of an appetite," Wily said, feeling a queasiness in the pit of his gut.

"Moshul was just making a mushroom-and-sprout salad," Lumina added. "I know you always like those."

Wily looked at his mother as if she had gone crazy. *What was she talking about?*

Then Wily heard a series of heavy footsteps approaching. He spun around—and saw none other than Moshul standing there, holding a wooden bowl of greens.

"Moshul!" Wily called out in disbelief.

He ran to the moss golem and threw his arms around one of his soft green legs. Roveeka hurried over and embraced his other leg. Odette was so excited that she vaulted off a chair and did a full body hug around his neck. Pryvyd, with Righteous floating by his side, stepped up behind the others.

Moshul seemed just as happy to see them. He put the salad bowl down on the nearby table and squeezed them all together in a long group hug.

"We thought we had lost you," Odette said, dropping back to the ground.

"How did you survive the fall?" Pryvyd spoke and signed at the same time.

Moshul signed back in response.

"My big brothers, the stone golems, are stronger than

I can ever be," Odette translated for Wily and Roveeka's benefit. "They are made of rock. But I am made of mud."

"That much I know," Pryvyd added, "but it doesn't answer my question."

"I think it does," Roveeka said with a big smile. "He's like a giant ball of wet clay." Roveeka was not the most mechanically inclined individual, but she was a brilliant geologist. She knew more about rocks, stones, and dirt than anyone else Wily had ever met.

"Then explain it to the rest of us," Pryvyd said to Roveeka.

"When a rock falls from a great distance," Roveeka said, "and strikes the hard ground, it shatters on its fault lines. It will break into a dozen pieces or more. But when clay hits the ground, if it's wet and moist enough, it doesn't break. It just changes shape."

Moshul nodded and then turned around with a look of embarrassment. His right shoulder and back, which were once muscular and impressive, now looked like a flat pancake covered in smashed lettuce. Moshul signed again, this time timidly.

"I know I look very silly," Odette translated for the moss golem. "Hopefully when the plants grow back on my shoulder, no one will notice."

"Who cares?" Wily said. "You're alive!"

"It doesn't matter what you look like," Roveeka said. "It's what's on the inside that counts."

"Which in your case is mud and worms," Odette said with a smirk.

"Some of the nicest worms around," Roveeka added.

"We're just so glad that you're here," Pryvyd said, with Righteous bobbing up and down in agreement at his side.

Wily thought that if Moshul had a mouth to smile with, he'd be doing so now. Instead, the golem's jeweled eyes just twinkled brightly.

Wily looked back to his mother as his stomach started to grumble. "All of a sudden," Wily said with a smile, "I am feeling very hungry."

# 5

## STEEL WALLS

That evening, a giant feast was held in the glass-floored dining room for Wily, his friends, and all the workers employed in the palace. A buffet was set with food for every palate, from roasted fish and watermelon salad to cricket stew and fungus spores. Just like every night, there was no wait staff serving the food. Each person helped themselves. It was one of the few traditions that Wily had brought from Carrion Tomb to the palace. He liked how it created a great sense of community, where everyone understood that no matter what their job was, they were all viewed as equals.

As the guests dined, the Skull of Many Riddles hovered around the room, assaulting people with its latest jokes. It floated over to the end of the table where Wily was sitting with Odette and Roveeka.

"A riddle for your amusement!" the skull cackled as its eye sockets burst into green flames.

Wily had tried to explain to the skull that terrifying the guests before telling a joke was not a good way to get a laugh, but for the levitating skull, old habits died hard.

"Go ahead," Wily said courteously.

"What does a crab dragon do before it goes to sleep?" the skull asked with a sinister grin.

Wily shrugged, even though he knew the answer.

"Eats his late-knight snack," the skull screamed victoriously.

Wily and Roveeka each squeezed out a polite chuckle. Odette didn't bother.

"Why aren't you roaring with laughter?" the skull moaned. "That was funny! Did you not understand it? There are two kinds of (k)nights. The kind with the sword and the kind at the end of the day with the moon. Ugh, these jokes are a much harder kind of riddle than I'm used to telling."

"Keep trying," Roveeka said, attempting to cheer the skull up. "You'll get the hang of it eventually."

∘⊙∘

WILY'S ATTENTION WANDERED. Nearby, Moshul, who had no mouth and didn't eat, had a small blanket laid on his outstretched legs, where Gremlin and Impish had set up a picnic for themselves with small portions of every treat. The two ferrets clinked a pair of tiny goblets together before diving into the food, making a crumby mess all over the blanket.

"Yecch," Roveeka said, her voice full of disgust.

Wily's focus was brought back to the table. His hobgoblet sister had pushed her dinner plate across the oak surface. A chunk of baked toad sat on the porcelain setting with only a small bite taken out of it.

"I thought baked toad was a hobgoblet delicacy," Wily said.

"It is," Roveeka responded, covering her mouth. "But this is horrible. So clean and fresh. It's lacking all the deliciously murky flavors that come with cooking it in a dirty pan and then letting it slowly rot for seven days."

"It tastes a lot like the toad we were served in Carrion Tomb to me," Wily said. Then he added, "But I don't have the refined tongue of a hobgoblet."

"You really don't," Roveeka agreed. "It's a wonder that I ever thought you were a hobgoblet at all." She looked down at her plate again. "Maybe if I add some slime mold." She reached for a small bottle on the table. "It might cover up the bright herb flavor."

She uncorked the bottle and let a puddle of gray slime dribble onto the toad. She picked up the chunk of meat and took another bite. Then she sighed, disappointed. "Didn't help."

Just then, from the far side of the hall, the drawbridge guard with silver face paint came racing in. She was chasing after a squatling that was no taller than her knee and had large yellow-and-black wings that would have seemed at home on the back of a giant tiger moth.

"Get back here!" the guard yelled as she tried to tackle the squatling.

The moth-winged creature flapped his wings and leaped high into the air. He grabbed hold of the bronze chandelier and hung there as he gasped for breath.

"I tried to stop him," the guard said apologetically to Wily, "but he was too fast. He refused to speak with anyone but you."

The squatling looked down from his perch. Wily could see that his brow was coated with sweat and his bare feet were blackened from hours of walking in the dirt. "I was told by the village elder to only talk with the prince," the squatling said.

"Go ahead," Wily called to him. "I'm listening."

"Last night, when the moon was still high," the squatling said, and Wily could hear the dread in his voice, "four stone golems came marching into Stilt Village, toppling houses and tossing carts. Many squatlings were injured. One nearly died."

A murmur of panic spread through the dining hall.

"Were the golems joined by anyone else?" Pryvyd asked.

"Yes. A pair of robed witches walked behind them."

"I don't understand," Odette blurted. "Of all the places in Panthasos . . . why attack Stilt Village? It's a quiet fishing town."

"I have an answer," the squatling said. "Although it is a strange answer indeed. The golems marched straight into town and ripped out the stone statue that stood at the center of our bubbling fountain. Then they marched off with it."

"They stole a statue?" Odette asked aloud. "Was it covered in diamonds or something?"

"No. It was just plain black stone. In fact, no one in Stilt Village liked it much at all."

"This statue . . . ," Wily asked. "What was it carved in the shape of?"

The squatling looked as if he were afraid to answer. "It was a statue of the Infernal King. Your father."

A hush fell over the dining room.

Lumina turned to Wily and, under her breath, whispered to him, "This is bad. Stalag and his mages are moving faster than we could have expected."

After a moment of silence, Wily stood up from the table. "Enjoy the rest of your dinner," he told the assembled guests as he started moving for the hall.

"Where are you going?" Roveeka asked.

"To my room. To think."

But Wily had a very different plan.

oOo

As his horse galloped along the dirt road that snaked through Trumpet Pass, Wily pulled his hooded cloak over his head and around his shoulders. He couldn't be sure if it was the chill in the air or the thought of seeing his father that was sending shivers down his arms.

Beyond the next cliff, he could see the steel walls of the prisonaut catching glints of moonlight in its polished surfaces. The prison on wheels had once rolled across the countryside, armed with gearfolk and snagglecarts, capturing the innocent and locking them within. But now, the prisonaut's wheels had been removed and it stood dormant at the foot of the Parchlands, holding captive just one man, a man that both his mother and Pryvyd would have discouraged Wily from visiting.

As Wily neared the imposing structure, a pair of soldiers came to the edge of the watchtower.

"This area is off-limits," the soldier called out. "Turn back."

Wily pulled the hood from his head, revealing his blue eyes and tangle of brown hair. "I'm here to see my father," he yelled back.

Upon clearly seeing his face, the soldiers recognized Wily. "Of course. Just give us a few minutes to prepare him for visitors."

Wily waited as the soldiers on the watchtower disappeared from view. He hadn't visited the prisonaut since defeating his father in the Infernal Fortress months earlier. His palms grew slick with sweat at the thought of this unpleasant reunion. It was enough to make him want to turn back and return to the royal palace without any answers as to why the statue had been stolen from Stilt Village. Before he could act upon his sudden hesitation, the sound of metal gears grinding against one another echoed through the valley. Wily watched as the gates of the prisonaut lifted open and a ramp descended.

On the other side of the steel wall, one of the soldiers stood waiting for him. "Right this way," the guard said.

The inside of the prisonaut was not what one would have expected from the outside. Instead of being filled with cages, it resembled a small town complete with cottages, street lamps, and a cobblestoned square. But it was still a prison. Along the tops of the walls, knights in silver armor patrolled with crossbows in hand.

"He's inside here," the guard said, stopping before a small, windowless house.

"I will speak with him alone," Wily said with a calm demeanor, despite feeling anything but calm.

"We've chained him down, so there's no need to worry," the soldier said as he opened the door to the cottage.

Wily walked inside and found himself in what appeared to be a small living room. Only instead of a couch and end tables, Wily's father sat in a wooden chair bolted to the floor, his ankles shackled to the legs.

Without his armor on, Kestrel Gromanov was a slight man, neither tall nor muscular. A pair of wire-rim spectacles sat on his nose like a crow perched on a branch. His hands lay in his lap with fingers interlocked, but his blue eyes tracked Wily as he crossed the room to a chair that was placed opposite him.

"It's not so easy, is it?" Kestrel said before Wily could take his seat.

"I don't know what you're talking about," Wily replied.

"Being king," Kestrel answered. "Holding the fate of the entire land in your hands. There are so many things that can go wrong. And everyone is looking to you for answers."

Wily sat silently as his father stared at him intently.

"I always enjoyed building things far more than giving commands," Kestrel said.

Wily swallowed hard. He felt the same way. Not that he was going to tell that to his father. They were nothing alike.

Except for their blue eyes. Wily couldn't help those.

"*You've* come to see *me*," his father spoke with an eerie calm. "I strongly doubt it's to count the wrinkles on my forehead."

"There was a statue of you in Stilt Village," Wily said. "It was stolen."

"Stolen?" Kestrel said. "How odd. That's not the kind of thing you can slip into your pocket when nobody's looking. It took a pair of my strongest snagglecarts to drag it there in the first place."

"It was ripped out of the ground by golems."

Wily waited for his father's reaction. After a long pause, a wide smile stretched across his face.

"Did you have something to do with this?" Wily asked. "Are you working with Stalag?"

"What would I do with a statue of myself?" Kestrel asked with a crooked smile. "How would that get me out of here? Unless, of course . . ."

"Unless what?" Wily was growing angry.

Kestrel mumbled something quietly to himself, then began to chuckle.

"Why are you laughing?" Wily got to his feet and moved closer to Kestrel. "What did you say?"

Suddenly, Kestrel moved swiftly. He darted forward and grabbed a screwdriver from Wily's trapsmith belt. In one fluid motion, he jammed the tip of the screwdriver into the locking mechanism of the cuffs holding his ankles in place. With a twist, the cuffs popped open, freeing Kestrel instantly.

Wily tried to bolt for the door of the cottage but his father was prepared. Kestrel snatched an ankle cuff off the floor and snapped one side of it around Wily's wrist and the other side to the chair Wily had been sitting on.

"Thanks for the screwdriver," Kestrel said with a smirk. "They don't let me have tools in here. They think I might do bad things with them."

"You won't get past the front gate," Wily said.

"I wouldn't be so sure," Kestrel snapped back. "In the dark of night, we look an awful lot alike." He pulled the cloak from Wily's shoulders and wrapped it around himself. "Which is why I'll be borrowing this too." He pulled his glasses off his face and pocketed them, then lifted the hood over his head and moved swiftly for the door. "Farewell."

Kestrel slipped out of the cottage, leaving Wily alone, wrestling to free his wrist from the tight cuff.

"The Infernal King is escaping!" Wily shouted at the top of his lungs.

It was impossible to know if anyone outside heard him at all.

Wily looked at the lock on the cuff. Even if he could have picked it, the only tool capable of doing the job had just been stolen by his father. He looked inside his trap-smith belt, desperate to find something else to set himself free. Then he spied a slender glass tube of lizard mucus.

*Ewww,* he thought. *But what choice do I have?*

With his free hand, he uncorked the tube of mucus and let globs of the slippery ooze drip down his trapped arm. Although disgusting, it made his arm as slippery as a wet rat. He twisted his wrist and tugged backward, pulling so hard that he nearly dislocated his thumb.

He tried again. With another tug, he was free.

Wily bounded from the chair and sprinted for the door. He grabbed its knob with his right hand, but his fingers were so slick with lizard mucus that they slipped off. He tried the knob again with his left. This time he was able to turn it.

Wily pushed open the door and spied, across the

courtyard, his cloaked father moving swiftly for the exit of the prisonaut—which was still wide open.

"Stop him!" Wily screamed.

The dozen knights patrolling the high walls looked down at Wily and then to the cloaked figure who was now hustling for the open gate. They all suddenly realized their mistake.

"Close it now!" one of the knights yelled.

Kestrel picked up speed, the hood fluttering off his head. He was steps away. If he got to Wily's horse—

With a mighty crash the gate came smashing down. Kestrel pulled to a halt, now trapped in the prisonaut. Soldiers quickly swarmed around him, pointing their crossbows at his chest.

"You can't blame me for trying," Kestrel said as the guards pulled the cloak from his shoulders.

"But you failed," Wily responded.

"I never lose," Kestrel retorted. "I just win later."

Wily narrowed his eyes, then asked his father a question still in need of answering. "What was so special about that statue?"

"It's made of neccanite," Kestrel said. "The strongest natural mineral. Only a diamond-tipped chisel could make the slightest dent in it. My engineers carved it from one of the few blocks of it ever found."

"But if Stalag found more," Wily concluded aloud, "he could build golems. Golems that no sword or ax could break."

"You are more clever than I give you credit for," Kestrel said. "But then again, you are my son. We have lots in common."

The knights began pulling Kestrel away, his hands now bound behind his back.

"Wait," Wily called to the knights. "He has my screwdriver."

The knights stopped Kestrel and patted him down, frisking him carefully for the stolen item. After a prolonged search, the soldiers stepped back empty-handed.

"There's nothing on him," one knight said.

"I must have dropped it," Kestrel said innocently.

Wily looked into his father's eyes.

"I told you," Kestrel said in a whisper, "I don't lose. I just win later."

Had this been what his father had intended from the moment Wily sat down opposite him? Not to escape now, but to steal Wily's screwdriver and hide it for some later purpose? Had Kestrel's run for the gate merely been a distraction from his true plan?

"We'll find the screwdriver," the knight said as he tugged Kestrel away.

Wily had a terrible feeling that the knights wouldn't find it until it was too late.

He'd discovered the secret of the statue but he wondered at what cost. Even after Kestrel was pulled out of view, Wily felt like he could still see his father's haunting smile.

# 6

# THE LEGEND OF PALOJAX

By the time Wily returned to the royal palace, the dining room was nearly empty. Only his closest companions were still gathered around the table impatiently awaiting his arrival. They all turned to him as he entered.

"Stalag is going to use the enchanted compass and the statue from Stilt Village to sniff out neccanite," Wily announced as he approached the table. "If he finds enough of the black stone, he will be able to mold it into an army of unstoppable golems."

"Just like the ones that marched across Panthasos when my grandparents were children," Lumina said before slumping back in her chair, defeated. "This is worse than I feared. Every elf, gwarf, and Knight of the Golden Sun standing together couldn't topple a dozen regular stone golems. Let alone ones made of neccanite."

"We could build our own army of golems," Roveeka said.

"It is a skill that only the cavern mages have," Pryvyd countered, "and every one of them will stand against us. They have been studying in their dungeons and catacombs, waiting for the moment to return to the surface and reclaim the Above. It's clear Stalag has declared that the time is now."

"There has to be a way to stop neccanite golems," Wily said. "If there were an army of them before, they must have been defeated somehow."

"They weren't stopped by man," Lumina said. "They were stopped by a beast. Not any ordinary beast: Palojax, the lair beast. A three-headed creature with a tail that can shatter mountains."

"A lair beast?" Odette said. "I thought that was a myth used to scare young elves into doing their chores."

"It is no myth," Lumina said. "My own mother saw the mighty Palojax when she was a child. She said that it made a full-size lobster dragon look as tiny as a dust mouse."

"Myth or no myth," Odette said, "all the lair beasts are gone now."

"Not gone," Lumina said. "Just hiding."

"Hiding?" Odette said with a laugh. "Where could a three-headed beast as tall as a great pine hide? There's no forest or hillside that they could call their home."

"Palojax is said to have found a peaceful haven that

few can reach," Lumina said. "A secret world beneath the deepest cave, a place known as the Below."

"I've never heard of it," Odette said.

"I have," Roveeka said with a gleam of excitement. "The Below is a place hobgoblets tell one another about. A place where the sun shines up. A place where wishes are granted."

"Yes, I remember," Wily said. "The elder hobgoblets would tell us to whisper our wishes to a piece of pyrite and throw it into the bottomless hole. They said the wish would travel all the way down into the Below. And if a hobgoblet was lucky, their wish would be granted by the upside-down star."

"A wish on an upside-down star?" Odette asked. "That sounds like the most ridiculous myth of all."

"I made a wish once," Wily said, gesturing to every-thing around him. "And it came true."

"The Below is real," Lumina said. "And so is Palojax."

"That's our answer, then," Pryvyd said. "If the lair beast is still there, we need to lure him back to the sur-face to save Panthasos."

Everyone around the dining table began to murmur.

"Unfortunately, a lair beast is not like a mercenary for hire or a noble knight," Lumina countered. "Palojax is still a beast, no matter how much good it's done in the past. It will not come to our aid willingly."

"Then why did it stop the golems last time?" Wily asked.

"Beast quellers led it into battle," Lumina answered. "The most trained and gifted members of the Roamabout tribe were able to control it long enough to rid the world of the neccanite golems."

"You're a beast queller, right?" Roveeka said, hopefully. "You were a member of the Roamabout tribe. That's what Epenya Veldt, the squatling we met in the Twighast Forest, told us when we were searching for you."

"As talented as I am," Lumina said, "I was never trained in the ancient art of controlling lair beasts. Every creature must be calmed in their own manner. It's an incredibly difficult skill that the elders never thought would need to be taught again."

"There must be somebody who knows how," Wily said, filled more with hope than certainty.

"Yes," Lumina said. "There are two. The nearly blind Olgara and her most talented student, a young girl named Valor Pelage. The knowledge is passed down from generation to generation. When I left to become the Scarf, Olgara was teaching it to Valor just as my great-grandmother had taught it to her."

"That's great. I'm sure both of them will help us," Roveeka said.

"All we need is one," Lumina said. "But it may not be as easy as that. When I was living with the Roamabouts, they didn't like outsiders. They didn't trust them."

"Well, they haven't met me," Roveeka said with a crooked smile. "I'm very likable."

"Let me get this straight," Odette turned to Lumina. "You're suggesting that we seek out a blind sage and her student, hoping that they know the secret to a nearly impossible ancient art. Then convince them to join us on a deadly mission. And if that goes well, we still need to find the entrance to the Below, a mythical place with an upside-down star, and then come face-to-face with a beast so fierce that neccanite golems would back away in fear?"

"That about sums it up," Lumina said, clearly realizing how daunting it sounded.

A stillness fell over the hall, a quiet so intense that it made Wily wonder if his ears had suddenly stopped working.

"It sounds like a wonderful plan," Roveeka said.

"I think it's crazy," Odette said.

"What do you think, Wily?" Pryvyd asked. "You're the future king."

Suddenly, every head in the room turned toward Wily.

*Why do I have to make this decision?* Wily thought to himself. *I'm just a trapsmith. I shouldn't be in charge. I never asked for all this responsibility.*

He could feel his throat closing under the pressure. *Is this a good plan? Or is it just a fool's errand with no hope of success? The decision I make will affect all of Panthasos. The lives of thousands of men, women, and children are in my hands.*

Wily sat there, staring down through the translucent floor at the kitchen below. It felt as if a pair of invisible hands were pushing down on his shoulders with such force that he might break through the glass floor of the dining room and go tumbling down to where the chefs were cleaning the dishes. He had to say something. He had to make a decision.

"I think we should try to find the lair beast," Wily said, his voice cracking.

"Are you sure?" Odette asked, sensing his hesitation.

"I'm certain," Wily said.

But the only thing Wily was certain of was that he wasn't certain about anything at all.

oOo

HAVING LEFT BEFORE dawn, Wily and his companions were treated to a glorious sunrise over the Eastern Gorge. But even the swath of orange and pink didn't lift his spirits.

Odette, always the morning elf, called over to Wily from her neighboring horse. "I think that's proof that sunrises beat sunsets every day of the week."

Roveeka, who had taken her favorite spot on Moshul's shoulders, nodded in agreement.

Lumina, who was at the head of the group, led them

over the next rise, giving Wily a clear view of the Parchlands. It was a strange sight to behold. Much of the Parchlands were long plains of browned grass and dusty rocks, but thanks to Wily and his knack for engineering, cutting through it were snakes of emerald-green vegetation. An extended drought had left the once fertile farmland barren and lifeless, but Wily, along with a team of locksage engineers and gwarven builders, had constructed a new network of aqueducts. Now there were giant stone rivers elevated in the sky, built to deliver water from the high streams far down to the dry farmlands.

"Quite a feat of construction," Pryvyd said, looking out at the aqueducts, his new spiked shield hanging at his side. "Something to feel proud of."

Wily tried to squeeze out a smile, but he kept thinking about all the people who were counting on him to stop Stalag and the army of stone golems the cavern mages were building. It made his stomach flip like a turtle under a waterfall.

As they galloped toward the first snake of green, Wily could see a magnificent rainbow stretching beneath the length of the aqueduct. Wily had engineered it so that a gentle spray of water would shoot out from the large pipes all along their path. It had been tricky to design a system that delivered just enough water to allow plants to grow. If too much shot from the aqueducts, the entire field would flood and turn into an uninhabitable swamp of thick mud. So far, the experiment had been a success.

"What's wrong?" Roveeka asked Moshul as he slowed to a halt behind Wily.

Moshul bent down and put his head against the ground, listening. Everyone pulled their horses to a stop. The moss golem could hear vibrations in the mud and stone. It was almost as if the ground could tell him things. After a moment, Moshul lifted his head and began to sign.

Pryvyd translated. "He hears frantic feet pounding against the earth. People running in fear."

Moshul pointed to a cluster of cottages and barns beyond the first six aqueducts. Righteous didn't waste a moment. It pulled the sword from Pryvyd's sheath and flew off.

"Wait up!" Pryvyd shouted at his departing arm. "Don't make me tie a leash to you."

Pryvyd snapped the reins of his horse and galloped after Righteous. Wily and the others were quick to follow. They raced under the first aqueduct and through the gentle mist that sprayed down. As their path took them through five more, Wily could feel his shirt soak with water.

Ahead, he saw the small town was in a state of chaos. Farmers and their families were running from houses and shops as a swarm of slither trolls bashed open doors and tore open shutters.

"This place looks good for me," a slither troll with a long, crooked nose shouted as he stuck his head into a farmhouse. "Plenty of room for all my clubs and my pet rats."

"I'm taking this one," another slither troll said as she started carving a deep gash in the wooden door of a cottage with her fingernail. "And the cottage next door too."

"They're not yours to take," a farmer shouted as she swung a rake at the invading slither trolls.

"This will all be ours soon," the long-nosed troll replied, snatching the tool from the farmer's hand.

The slither troll was about to swing the rake at the terrified woman when Righteous flew across and blocked the blow with a sword.

"Go back to the dungeon you crawled out of," Odette called as she vaulted off her horse.

With a handspring, she leaped to the side of the farmer and snatched a shovel from the ground. But it soon became clear that defending the cottage would be too difficult; it was quickly surrounded by a dozen more trolls.

"Over here!" Roveeka said from her perch on Moshul's shoulders.

Moshul spread his legs, allowing Odette and the farmer to run through them. As soon as they were safely behind him, Moshul snapped his legs shut.

"They're going to take my house," the farmer said.

"This way," Odette insisted, taking the woman's hand and pulling her farther away from danger.

Wily and Lumina rode deeper into town to find dozens more slither trolls rampaging through the streets. Their slimy footprints painted the earth in a dizzying pattern of green and black.

"Where did they all come from?" Wily asked.

"I don't know, but I think *he* has something to do with it." Lumina gestured to an obese man in a tattered brown robe floating a few feet off the ground.

"From now on," the obese man yelled, "this town shall be called Girthbellow. For I am Girthbellow the Great."

The slither trolls in the town square cheered in celebration.

"As the Prince of Panthasos," Wily shouted in his most declarative voice, "I order you to leave."

"You won't be the prince of anything for much longer," Girthbellow chortled. "Stalag came to my catacomb. Told me the time of the magic-born has come at last. The stone golems will see to that."

"He spoke too soon," Odette said.

Righteous, Pryvyd, Odette, Moshul, and Roveeka came up behind Wily and Lumina.

"There's thirty-eight of us," Girthbellow chortled. "And I see just six of you."

Righteous raised its sword defiantly.

"Six and a quarter," Girthbellow corrected himself.

A dozen more slither trolls exited stores and cottages nearby.

"He's got a point," Odette whispered to Wily.

But Wily didn't hear what Odette had said. He had just noticed something peculiar. There was one portion of the town's marketplace that had no footprints at all—a wide circle surrounding a cart overflowing with cherry tomatoes.

"I've got an idea," Wily said. "Follow me."

Wily sprinted for the cart as the others chased behind him. Once within the circle, Wily pointed to the elastic tarp hanging over the nearby potato stall.

"Moshul, grab that," Wily said.

As Moshul pulled down the stretchy piece of cloth, Wily quickly turned to the others. "We had a slither troll in Carrion Tomb once. Despite being fierce and nasty, they have really sensitive skin. Especially to acidic things like amoebolith ooze, lichenberries—and, I'm hoping, cherry tomatoes."

"And you're planning on making them a salad?" Odette asked in disbelief.

"No," Wily said as Moshul handed him the tarp. "We're going to build a giant slingshot."

"To fire cherry tomatoes at the trolls?" Odette asked with even more disbelief.

The slither trolls neared, slicing the air with their black dagger-sharp fingernails.

Wily stretched the tarp across the back of the tomato cart, tying both ends in place. He loaded a dozen ripe fruit into the slingshot, pulled back, aimed at a pair of slither trolls, and fired.

The soft projectiles soared through the air and struck the trolls on their legs and bellies. The trolls both let out pained yelps. "Ohhh! That burns!" one screamed. "Ouch. Ouch. Ouchie."

The trolls turned and fled as Wily loaded the slingshot again. The other trolls ducked in fear as more tomatoes took to the sky and landed with explosive splatters on the ground.

"What are you doing?" Girthbellow screamed at the trolls as a cherry tomato smacked him in the side of the face.

The slither trolls ran from the town as Wily continued to slingshot the acidic fruit. The hovering Girthbellow looked around, realized this was a battle he couldn't win, and started to back away as well.

"We'll be back soon to claim this town," Girthbellow shouted as he was doused in bits of tomato pulp. "Once the golems march, it will be you who will be fleeing in terror."

Girthbellow turned and soared off after his slither troll minions. When they were gone, the farmers of the town came out from their hiding spots.

"You're safe now," Wily called to the people, proud that his ingenuity had saved the day.

No one smiled or clapped though. They all looked . . . angry.

"But for how long?" a farmer called out. "Throwing fruit at them isn't an answer."

"There's only so many tomatoes we can grow," another farmer yelled.

"We need a permanent solution to this," another townsperson called out.

Wily began to sweat as the angry farmers continued to challenge him.

"What are you going to do about it?" a farmer screamed. "You're just like your father."

"The Infernal King was wretched," another said, "but at least he kept the monsters away. You can't even do that."

"I'm on a quest to—"

"Great! A quest!" a farmer called out. "That doesn't sound very promising. While you're off adventuring, what happens to us?"

"We want a real king," an old man yelled. "Not a boy playing dress up. A real king would be able to protect us."

Lumina pulled Wily aside and spoke softly. "We should go. There's nothing you can say to these people right now."

"Your mom's right," Pryvyd seconded as he signaled for his horse.

Odette whistled for the other horses. Wily and his friends quickly got on their mounts.

"And now he's leaving," a farmer shouted.

"I promise that I will fix this," Wily called back as his horse began to canter out of the farm town.

As the group galloped off to the east, Wily could hear the sound of the people booing.

# STRANGE GUSTS

The farther they traveled along the low path through the Parchlands, the fewer people they saw. By the afternoon, the adventuring party finally came to the end of the dirt road. Wily's mind kept wandering back to the cruel words the farmer had spat at him. *A real king would be able to protect us.* It stung all the more because Wily thought it was true.

"Where's your smile?" Lumina asked as she rode up alongside Wily.

"It's still here," Wily said. "Just hiding, I guess." After a pause, he said, "You knew my father way better than I do. Are we alike?"

"Is that what this is about?" Lumina asked. "Don't take the farmers' words to heart. They were upset about their farms. People say mean things when they're stressed."

"You didn't answer my question," Wily replied.

His mother paused, thinking a beat too long. "You are not a mean person like your father. You would never hurt anyone."

"That doesn't mean I will make a good king, though," Wily stated.

More than anything else, he wanted his mother to tell him he would be the best king Panthasos had ever seen, but before she was able to respond, Odette came riding up alongside them. "Where do we go from here?" the elf asked.

Lumina pointed to an oddly shaped mountain jutting out from the tree line in the distance. Instead of its peaks pointing up toward the sky, the jagged rocks poked out from it in dozens of strange angles, like the spikes of a thorn-shelled turtle.

"We aim for the mountain known as the Web," Lumina said. "The Roamabout camp is usually within walking distance of its base, although the precise location changes frequently. Like the beasts they train, the tribe prefers to remain hidden."

"But you know how to find them?" Odette said.

"With Impish and Gremlin's keen noses," Lumina said, lowering her hands to the ferrets sticking their heads out of her saddlebags, "we shouldn't have too tough a time."

The two ferrets looked very pleased with themselves, happy to suddenly be important.

"If we keep up the pace we've been making so far,"

Lumina said, "we'll make it to the foot of the mountain before nightfall."

Lumina urged her horse forward, leaving Odette and Wily to stare at the strange mountain in the distance.

"I can't see why they named the mountain 'The Web,'" Odette said.

"It's not the strange shape that sparked the name," Pryvyd said as he joined the others. "The reason is below the tree line: a place called Spider Rock. I patrolled the area once with the Knights of the Golden Sun. It's swarming with beasts of all sorts."

Moshul signed to the others.

"No," Pryvyd said to Moshul, "I didn't see anything with tentacles. Relax."

Moshul did not seem comforted as Pryvyd departed. The moss golem signed to Odette.

"I don't think there is even a species of octopus that lives on the land," Odette responded. "We've got to get you over this fear."

Moshul bowed his head timidly, and Roveeka gave him a big hug around his neck.

"Even big guys are allowed to be afraid of some things," she said encouragingly.

oOo

UNLIKE SOME OF the dense thickets Wily and his companions had chopped their way through in the past, this forest consisted of giant trees whose trunks were spread so far apart that it was dozens of steps between their bases. Above, however, the mighty branches crossed over and through one another, leaving not a sliver of sky exposed. The late afternoon sun cast the forest floor in a soft green glow.

They had already been traveling through the woods for many hours when Wily felt a gentle breeze run through his tangle of brown hair. He saw that up ahead the woods opened to a glen of high grass. Lumina led them out into the open field.

"It's a field of feather grass," Lumina said, pointing to the wide blades of green, purple, and blue that shot up from the earth.

As the wind continued to blow, the field undulated like the wings of a bird flapping. Wily watched the field change colors as each blade caught the light from a slightly different angle. It amazed Wily how, even after months of being out of Carrion Tomb, there were still new sights to be seen in the Above.

Odette leaned down from her horse and grabbed a fistful of grass. She began sliding its blades into her hair as colorful decorations.

"You should grab some too," Odette said to Roveeka, who as usual was riding on Moshul's shoulders. "But probably not to stick in your hair. Because you don't have any."

"Some people weave them into crowns," Lumina said.

She was about to say more when her voice trailed off. She was staring at the feather grass on the far side of the field. Each stalk shook like a young hobgoblet about to perform her first ambush.

"Hold on!" Lumina shouted.

A gust of wind rushed at Wily with such force that it nearly knocked him off the back of his horse. He looked to the south, the direction from which the wind had come. All the trees beyond the edge of the glen were swaying back and forth as if shaken by the hands of an angry giant. Above the trees was a small pocket of gray, churning clouds.

"It's a small wind storm," Pryvyd said, "and it appears that it's blowing in our direction."

"We need to get out of this field fast," Lumina said with rising panic. "At least in the forest we can hide."

"Hide?" Roveeka asked. "I thought storms don't follow people. Aren't they just—what did you call it again?" Roveeka thought for a second. "Weather?"

"Most storms just blow where the wind takes them," Lumina said, "but that's not a normal storm. That's the trail of a monsoonodon."

"Monsoonodon?" Odette asked. "That's a mouthful. Talk about an animal that needs a nickname."

"I've never heard of this creature," Pryvyd said.

"You wouldn't have unless you'd lived in these parts," Lumina said, giving an urgent nudge to her horse. "They are giant furry beasts with long tusks that spark like lightning bolts. Their footsteps churn the wind into a fury. A shake of their fur causes torrential downpours. And judging from the size of that cloud, this is a big one."

Lumina took off across the glen. The other horses raced behind her. Moshul hurried to keep up with the others as they galloped for the distant tree line.

"The beast quellers calmed the monsoonodons a long time ago," Lumina continued, "and brought them to a safe mountain valley where they can live in peace. The storms they cause form the famous Pago-Pago Falls."

"If they're all kept in that valley," Wily asked, "what's one doing down here?"

"I can only guess that something disturbed them," Lumina said. "We should make sure to keep our distance. They are fierce and nearly unstoppable when they're storming. Even a whole team of quellers can have difficulty calming them."

Wily felt the wind getting stronger as the clouds swept closer. Although he couldn't see the creature yet, he certainly could hear its booming thunder steps and the crackle of trees being split in half. All the birds and insects hidden in the feather grass took flight, soaring into the sky in a burst of panic.

Then, out of the corner of his eye, Wily watched as a pair of enormous trees snapped from their stumps and got tossed in the air like brittle twigs. A moment later, a giant hoofed beast three times as tall as a horse and many times wider blasted out of the forest. Its wet gray coat twinkled in the last rays of sunlight that were about to vanish in the dark clouds that followed the creature. Four long tusks extended from either side of its snout, electricity arcing from the tip of one to the next. As the creature exited the forest, it let out a bellowing snort that caused the clouds overhead to spin like a whirlpool in an underground lake.

The monsoonodon did not take long to spot Wily and his companions speeding across the field. It let out another loud snort and charged after them. Wily gave a sharp nudge to his horse, which really didn't need much encouragement to flee from the giant beast.

Righteous, with sword clutched, bravely hovered behind, prepared to take on the monsoonodon single-handedly (which of course was the only way Righteous could fight).

"Come on, Righteous!" Pryvyd called. "What do you think you're going to do? That sword would barely scratch its hide."

"For something so big and heavy," Wily asked Lumina, "how is it moving so fast?"

"It doesn't really matter how it's doing it," Odette said from the neighboring horse. "Just that it is. And that it's coming after us."

A thunderous boom was followed by the fresh scent of electrically charged ions floating through the air. Wily had once made a trap with winged shock eels, and he had loved the fragrant odor they would give off with each electrical zap.

The gusts caused by the monsoonodon were so strong now that Wily's horse was beginning to wobble. For a moment, his steed was even lifted off the ground, its hooves scrambling to find the safety of solid earth. A second later, his horse got his wish when he came down with a thud.

"We're not going to make it," Roveeka shouted to Moshul.

The moss golem was running so fast that his leg funguses were popping with every step, leaving puffs of purple smoke behind. Wily looked back to see if the toxic mushroom smoke would knock out the monsoonodon, but the strong breeze swirling around the beast simply blew the smoke away from its nostrils.

Lumina turned her horse in a wide semicircle.

"You go on," she called to Wily. "Your mission is too important."

"Lumina, no!" Pryvyd shouted at her. "What can you do to stop it?"

"I can distract it," Lumina said. "Give you just enough time to escape."

Lumina clapped her hands over her head. The monsoonodon changed direction, charging for Lumina. The powerful gusts blowing off the beast knocked her off her feet and into a tree. In moments, she would be trampled.

But before the beast reached her, a shrill chorus of voices arose from the adjacent woods.

"YOP-YOP-YOP-YOP!"

Seconds later, dozens of forest animals came stampeding out of the woods with humans and elves riding them like steeds. A tall woman rode on the back of a great green bear, clutching its fur in her fingers. Two elves rode in tandem on the shoulders of a majestic stag, gripping its antlers like handlebars. A trio of younger children sat on the scaly back of a giant rattlesnake. Many of the riders held long rods with hunks of food dangling from them like giant fishing poles. Others swung rope lassos overhead.

The woman on the bear and a man riding a flightless bird came charging at the monsoonodon from either side. Then, together, they began to *sing* to it. Wily couldn't believe his ears, nor could he hear the words of the song. Then again, with the wind blasting in his ears he could barely hear the hoof steps of his own horse.

Whatever the riders were singing, the monsoonodon didn't like it. It swung its head wildly, causing a downpour of rain so heavy that it felt as if small rocks were dropping from the sky. Its giant tusks swished toward the head of the bear rider. At the last second, the rider dropped to the side of the beast, gripping its mane in her fingers. Her heels dragged across the earth as the monsoonodon's tusks went tearing overhead in a shower of sparks.

"Steer clear of here!" a man riding on the back of a mammoth dog called out to Wily and his companions.

Another group of animal riders came charging out of the woods in front of the creature. It quickly became clear that the first batch of riders had been corralling the monsoonodon into a trap. The riders who'd just emerged from the woods all began chanting in unison as they waved their arms up and down.

The monsoonodon slowed as it approached the wall of animals and people, but rather than stopping or barreling through the barricade, the shaggy beast changed direction and started straight for Wily and Moshul.

It hit the moss golem straight in the back. Moshul was knocked off his feet, and Roveeka went flying off his shoulders. But Moshul caught her in his mud hands before she struck the ground headfirst.

Wily gave a powerful pat to the side of his horse, encouraging him to run faster. Unfortunately, the pat was not enough. The horse was slammed hard by the monsoonodon. Wily was knocked from his saddle and hit the earth with a painful thump. Despite its name, the feather grass was no softer than any other grass.

Wily looked up to see the monsoonodon turning back to charge him yet again. He leaped to his feet. Panic flashed through him as his horse fled in fear.

*What can I do?* Wily thought. *There must be some way to stop that thing.* His mind flashed through everything he kept stored in his trapsmith belt. Unfortunately, it didn't include a giant stone wall—and even that might not have been enough to slow this beast of wind and rain. Wily was running out of ideas fast when, seemingly out of nowhere, a girl who looked about Wily's age, on top of a black-and-gold mountain lion, came riding up beside the beast. She leaped from her lion onto the back of the monsoonodon and, with one fluid motion, slid down over the forehead of the beast until her belly was pressed up against the beast's snout. She landed with her feet propped up against the beast's lightning tusks.

The monsoonodon was still charging at Wily, looking past the young girl standing on its face. Wily couldn't hear if she was speaking, but he could see that she had her hands firmly gripped on the beast's eyelids and was staring directly into its eyes. Despite the wind and rain pummeling her, she didn't let go.

Wily watched the beast slow to a stop as the girl petted the top of its head calmly. Only after the monsoonodon was lying on its belly did the rest of the riders encircle the beast. Now, in unison, they all began to chant. After a minute of quiet singing, the beast was smiling happily, the downpour had diminished to a gentle drizzle, and the wind had stilled.

The girl hopped off the head of the monsoonodon and approached Wily. She was barefoot and wore a skirt that looked as if it had been woven from slices of tree bark and vine string. As she got closer, Wily could see that she had large brown eyes and light olive-colored skin. She carried herself with an unmistakable air of confidence. "It's not safe for wall-dwellers to be this far out in the wilds," the girl said.

"Wall-dwellers?" Wily asked.

"People who choose to sleep under roofs and between stone walls rather than beneath nature's canvas."

"We owe you great thanks," Wily said.

"I'm just glad you didn't get yourself trampled," she said. "Henrietta can brew up quite a storm. Let me introduce myself. I'm Valor Pelage, Quellmaster of the Roamabouts."

"That's amazing," Wily said, his voice and his heart filled with hope. "We were just coming to you for help."

"What is it that you want of . . ."

Valor's words trailed off as she spotted Lumina limping over from where she'd fallen. The girl's expression suddenly changed, twisting into a storm of emotions. Her eyes cold, she stepped past Wily and toward Lumina.

"Is he a friend of yours?" Valor asked, pointing to Wily.

"He's my son," Lumina responded with some hesitation.

"That's even worse. So much worse."

# VALOR

"You abandoned the tribe and the people you cared about," Valor said, her voice bitter as acid. "And now you have the nerve to return asking for help?"

Lumina slowly approached Valor as if moving toward a fang orc that could bite at any moment.

"The wall-dwellers aren't bad," Lumina said, the words leaving her lips like cautious cave lemmings. "They're just different."

"You married the Infernal King," Valor said, her voice rising. "Maybe you're not such a great judge of character."

"He wasn't the Infernal King when I married him," Lumina replied. "He was a good man who got lost when he sat on a throne."

This last comment only served to make Valor angrier. "He burned down forests without thinking about the innocent animals living inside. How can you even think of defending him?"

"He did horrible things. Which is why I spent the last decade fighting him."

"No one has heard from you in years," Valor spat back. "Where were you? Hiding in the shadows? Or crawling like a squirrel in a tree?"

"I was disguised behind many colored scarves."

Valor's eyes went wide. If she was mad before, now she was ready to belch flames. "You were the Scarf? I fought alongside you during the second battle of the Twighast! And you never said a thing! How could you be so callous? I used to call you Auntie."

All of the other Roamabouts stood silently, taking in this surprising revelation. Even the monsoonodon seemed to be listening to every word.

"I needed everyone to believe I was dead," Lumina explained. "If the Infernal King thought I was still alive, I was worried he would hold the Roamabouts hostage until I turned myself in."

"You could have told me," Valor said. "I could have kept a secret."

"The Infernal King's rust fairies were everywhere. Spying."

"I thought you were dead," Valor said, tightening her jaw.

"I knew that you would become the strong girl you are today."

Valor looked over to Wily with scorn. All the warmth and kindness she had shown upon first meeting him dissipated instantly. Valor stared at him as if he were the Infernal King himself.

"You will get no help from me," Valor said. "And I will strongly discourage any other member of the tribe from helping you. Go back to your castle of stone and metal. Leave the trees and rivers to us. We'll do just fine without you."

Valor turned away from Wily and his companions. "Stalkeer!" she shouted.

Her black-and-gold mountain lion bounded up to her side. She jumped on the great cat's back, and together they disappeared into the trees.

A tall elf riding on the back of a great stag was the first to speak. "You are welcome to come to our camp and rest. But then you must swiftly continue on your way."

Wily could see that his mother was too choked up with emotion to say anything at all. Despite his own tumultuous feelings, he spoke in her place. "Thank you," Wily replied. "We would appreciate that."

The tall elf turned to the Roamabouts on the back of the giant snake. "Take Henrietta back to Pago-Pago Valley."

The three Roamabouts nodded and approached the monsoonodon. They gently nudged it to its feet and started leading it toward a break in the forest. The tall elf on the stag rode in a different direction. She beckoned Wily and the others to follow her.

"Why did Valor call you Auntie?" Wily asked his mother once they had mounted their horses and were following the strange cavalcade of animals and their Roamabout riders through the pathless woods.

"Her mother and father died when she was little. She was raised by the tribe. But our relationship was always especially close. Until I left. I'd rather not talk about it." Lumina rode ahead without another word.

As the procession twisted through the mighty trees, Wily watched as the woodling animals peeked out of their burrows and down from their nests. They chirped, tweeted, and hissed their respect for the passing quellers.

After an hour's ride, the companions emerged from the woods into a field of saplings no taller than a horse's head. Wily was now able to get a much clearer view of the mountain known as the Web. While it was a magnificent sight to behold, the large rock formation at its base was even more breathtaking. It was shaped like a giant spider. Eight pillars of stone held aloft an enormous boulder high above the lush mountainside. Mossy trees and thick shrubs grew in the shade of the great tower of stone shaped by wind and erosion.

Wily couldn't take his eyes off the giant spider as they crossed through the field of saplings. Only after his view was blocked by a cluster of gargantuan elms did he notice the smell of roasting vegetables wafting through the air. The scent grew stronger as they approached the clearing, which held the campsite of the Roamabout tribe.

Wily discovered quickly that there wasn't much to the campsite. There were no cabins or tents or even sleeping mats, just pillows laid out on the soft grass and small bonfires set up to cook food and provide warmth. There were at least three times as many animals wandering the camp as there were people. A stream passed through the far side of the clearing, where a trio of beavers was busy building a dam as squatlings fished in the waters.

Wily could now see the source of the fragrant smell of roasting vegetables. A group of tinder frogs had been gathered in the middle of a ring of rocks. Their backs crackled with a warm fire. Spits of mushrooms and crispy crickets cooked on skewers above them. The tinder frogs happily snatched curious mosquitoes and gnats from the air with their long tongues as the food cooked.

Roamabouts looked up as Wily and his companions passed. Not a single one offered a smile to the newly arriving visitors.

"Find yourself a rock or patch of grass to sit upon," the tall elf said to Wily and his companions. "Or if you are hungry, there is plenty to eat. Once you have rested, you can make your way to a town with your kind."

Impish and Gremlin bounded from Lumina's saddle-bag and scampered over to a family of ferrets. Whether they knew each other from before or were making introductions was unclear to Wily, but either way they all seemed happy to be together.

The tall elf turned to Lumina. "I can think of only one person who will be happy to see you again. And here he comes now."

As the tall elf walked off, a broad-shouldered man with a face that resembled not only Lumina's, but Wily's, bounded up to the just-arriving group.

"My goodness!" he exclaimed. "I can't believe it! But then again, when were you not full of surprises?"

Lumina gently descended from her mount, and the two embraced. The man looked up and saw Wily, still on his horse. "So you found each other," the man said with a smile. He released Lumina and came over to Wily's horse. "I'm your uncle Talleywin. You look just like your grandfather did. Same chin, same hair, and same ears. Just the eyes are different. Those must be from the other side of the family."

"I'm very glad to meet you," Wily said. "We haven't had the warmest welcome so far."

"It's to be expected," Talleywin said. "No one here trusts a wall-dweller. Much less a member of the royal family. Not after what the Infernal King did to the land."

"I would never destroy the forests," Wily said. "Or any other part of nature."

"You'll have a tough time convincing anyone here of that," Talleywin replied. "Your kind believes in order and control. We believe in freedom and the beautiful chaos of the wild."

Talleywin gave a wide smile, but Wily could tell that, despite them being blood relatives, his uncle eyed him with a sense of caution.

"Now tell me what you are doing in the shadow of the Web," Talleywin asked Lumina.

She proceeded to explain in great detail. Talleywin listened carefully until she finished.

"Tame Palojax?" Talleywin had to restrain himself from laughing. "Only Valor has been trained in the ancient art. And she won't even speak with you, let alone journey to the Below by your side."

"I'll change her mind," Wily said. "I have to."

"That's a task even more unlikely than reaching the lair beast alive," Talleywin stated. "Once Valor makes up her mind, the conversation is over."

"What about Olgara?" Lumina asked. "Is she still well? Perhaps she would go with us."

"She spends all her time now in her perch," Talleywin replied. "Not sure she would be able to do much adventuring. She can barely see. But you can ask her yourself."

Lumina turned to Odette, Roveeka, Moshul, Righteous, and Pryvyd.

"I think it would be best if you stayed here," she said. "We don't want to give her any extra reason to say no."

The others settled in as Talleywin guided Wily and Lumina across the clearing to the edge of the stream and hopped across the rocks. He stepped into the woods on the other side.

"Olgara doesn't live here with you?" Wily asked, confused.

"She doesn't like people much anymore," Talleywin answered. "Not that she ever did. She only cares about discovering new breeds of birds and bugs."

Talleywin continued into the woods as Wily and Lumina crossed the stream to catch up. They were rather curious woods; all around, Wily could hear chirps and squeaks of rodents and birds, yet when he peered through the dense foliage, he couldn't see any animals at all. He wondered if they blended into the surroundings like the camouflaging lizards that stuck to the walls of Carrion Tomb. He heard the forest noises grow louder as they approached a large elm, but when he peeked around the other side of the tree, once again he saw nothing at all. Wily concluded that either a powerful magic was at work or these animals were practically invisible.

Talleywin slowed as he approached a giant tree with a waist-tall hole in the trunk.

"She lives in there?" Wily asked.

"No," Talleywin answered. "She lives up high." He pointed into the branches above. "This is just how we get there."

Talleywin ducked and crept into the base of the tree, disappearing inside. Wily hesitated briefly, then followed behind.

Once inside, he was treated to a wondrous sight. The giant tree was hollow from its base to the sky. And it was teeming with life. Birds flew loops from one side to the other. Squirrels and tree rats scampered up the inner bark. Wily suddenly realized where all the sounds had been coming from.

"By the look on your face," Talleywin said, "I'm guessing you've never been inside a hollow tree before. The whole forest is full of them."

Wily peered up at the sky through the hole at the top of the tree. Then he looked around for ladders or steps to climb.

"How do we get up there?" Wily asked, puzzled.

Talleywin pointed to discs of blue fungus sticking out from the inside tree bark. They trailed up and around the tree like a giant spiral staircase—but with no banister.

"Are those strong enough to hold our weight?" Wily asked with a healthy amount of skepticism.

"I wouldn't jump on them," Talleywin replied, an answer that didn't exactly put Wily at ease.

"You'll be fine," Lumina said, "as long as you take each one slowly."

Talleywin started to climb the fungus steps, Wily and Lumina following. Wily was not afraid of heights.

He had run along the edge of the bottomless pits of Carrion Tomb without fear. These steps, however, were far more nerve-racking. Each plate of fungus bent gently when weight was put on it. It gave Wily the sickly sensation that they could break off at any moment.

"Just keep looking up," Lumina said to him as she climbed cautiously, favoring her injured leg. Wily took her advice and tried to focus on the colorful birds that fluttered past his head as they circled to the top of the tree.

When they finally reached the top, they were not treated to the incredible view Wily had expected. Instead, they found themselves in a dense canopy of branches that blocked any kind of vista.

Talleywin stopped and tweeted to a small bird. It tweeted back a response.

"This way," he said, walking along a slender branch and using other, higher branches to help keep his balance.

Wily followed behind. After a short distance, he could see an old woman sitting on a limb with her bare feet dangling. This had to be Olgara!

She was weaving a small nest of twigs and straw. As they approached, she looked up and pulled a slice of wet straw from her cracked lips. "You stay there," she called out. "I'll come to you."

Olgara dropped from the limb. Wily gasped as she grabbed the branch with her hands and climbed underneath it. For someone old and wrinkled, it was startling to see her move with such agility. With a powerful swing, she hoisted herself back to the top of the branch.

"Just built a new pollenpuffer nest," Olgara said. "Don't need you knocking it over."

"This is Lumina's son," Talleywin said. "Wily Snare."

"Hmmm," Olgara said, "the future King of Panthasos. Was wondering when you'd crawl up my tree. Was sure you were not dead."

Olgara bounded forward and grabbed Wily by the hands and pulled them close to her eyes. She examined his fingers as if there were words written on his skin.

"You've already done your fair share of beast quelling," Olgara said, as she slid the tips of her knobby fingers along the palms of his hands.

"What makes you say that?" Wily said as her fingernails tickled his skin.

"I recognize many of these scars and nicks," Olgara said as she pressed his hands so close to her nose that his knuckles rubbed up against her bushy eyebrows. "This looks like the bite of a ghost spider. Here is the burn mark from a hungry ooze beast. And I noticed the ink stains beneath your fingernails. What was that from? A lake octopus?"

"A giant cave squid, actually," Wily said, impressed by her many accurate guesses.

"A particularly grumpy breed," she said as she rubbed his forearm along her cheek. "I'm surprised I don't feel suction cup scars all down your arms."

"You mean like these?" Wily asked.

Wily rolled up his pant leg to reveal a very faint trail of circles that extended from his inner thigh down to his ankle.

She bent down and pressed her eyes up to them. "Where did you encounter all of these strange creatures?"

"I spent my whole childhood underground in a dungeon known as Carrion Tomb."

"Very dangerous beasts for an untrained boy to be dealing with," Olgara said. "You must have your mother's natural touch."

"Olgara," Lumina said. "We need you to come with us to quell the lair beast Palojax."

The blind woman shook her head and brushed off the request. "Oh no," she mumbled. "No more quelling for me. Just making nests and teaching young quellers. You'll need to find someone else."

"There is nobody else," Lumina said. "The safety of Panthasos is at stake."

"Cities may crumble. Towns may burn. But grass will grow in the ashes."

She was about to swing away when Wily spoke up. "You don't need to go. Train me."

"Train you to quell a lair beast! Impossible."

"You just said yourself he has natural talent," Lumina reminded her.

"But natural talent alone is not a replacement for

practice." Olgara grabbed a big leaf of a tree branch and shoved it in her mouth. After some noisy chewing, she spoke again. "You would need ten years of lessons every day to even have a chance."

"We only have until tomorrow," Lumina said. "Or the next day at the most."

Olgara spat out the leaf.

"I might surprise you," Wily added timidly, not really believing it himself.

"What exactly have you been told about Palojax?" Olgara asked as bits of mulch flew from her lips.

It suddenly occurred to Wily that he didn't know much at all about the lair beast. "I know that lair beasts are very large."

"Yes, they are big," Olgara said. "Much bigger than the largest dragon. But it is not size that makes them so difficult to quell. Palojax is not just one beast but a stew of many. It has the body of a giant lizard and the wings of a bat. It has six legs of a giant insect and a tail of an ankylosaur. But most important to the quelling process is that lair beasts have three heads—that of a snake, a bear, and a frightclops. Each head needs to be quelled without upsetting the other two. The tricks that work on one won't work on the others. You can't use song or hand motions or command words to calm them."

"But there is a way?" Wily asked.

"Yes," Olgara said after a long pause. "There is a way. Direct pressure to the spot where the necks join up to form one spine. But that requires being on top of them. And if you get it wrong, Palojax will only grow angrier. The heads will rip you to pieces, each wishing to devour you on its own."

"I need to try," Wily begged, despite the sudden feeling that he wanted to run back to the royal palace. "Stone golems are already marching across Panthasos. Palojax is the only way to stop them."

"Even if I showed you the technique," Olgara scoffed, "there are no lair beasts to practice on. It would be impossible to know if you're even doing it right."

"What about the manticorn?" Lumina asked. "It has more than one head just like the lair beast. Is there still one that lives above Spider Rock?"

Talleywin nodded. "As far as I know."

"Please," Wily said. "Teach me. I'm begging you."

Olgara snapped off a slender branch and stuck it in her mouth. She crunched on it until the pulp filled the gaps between her teeth. "I will give you one day of training. Only to prove how little you know."

# 9

## PRESSURE POINTS

"The beasts of the wild are like mirrors that peer into your heart," Olgara said as she shuffled along an elm branch that extended into a neighboring tree's foliage. "If you are angry, they will return that anger. If fear is in your heart, you will see a reflection of that same trepidation in the beast's eyes."

Wily had been following Olgara through the treetops for the last hour as she talked. As far as Wily could tell, she had yet to give him a single piece of practical advice on how to quell a lair beast or any creature at all for that matter.

Olgara stepped off the elm branch into a curtain of pine needles and continued, "A beast responds to strength, but not the kind of strength found in your arms or legs or chest. It searches for a deeper strength."

As Wily joined Olgara in the pine tree, she poked him in the shoulder. "What is this?" she questioned.

"My shoulder?" Wily asked, flinching from the jab.

"Why is it so tight?" she replied, poking him again.

"Maybe I need to stretch?"

"No," she snapped back. "That is not what makes them tight. Tell me about your life. What worries you?"

"Normal stuff, I guess," Wily said, not understanding at all what she was getting at.

"No," she grabbed his shoulders, squeezing them. "I can feel this is new. Tell me about life in the palace."

"It's wonderful," Wily said. "Everyone cares about me. I have many friends. I don't have to sweep the floor all day." Then, after a pause, he added, "Although, I do have responsibilities."

"There," Olgara said victoriously. "Your shoulders just raised an inch. Tell me more about these responsibilities."

"Being the future king is a lot of pressure," Wily said. "A lot of people are counting on me."

"I can sense your shoulders rising with every word," Olgara said as she studied him closely, her wrinkled eyes inches from his cheekbone. "Keep talking."

Wily swallowed hard. This wasn't something he had ever discussed out loud before. "I guess sometimes the palace walls make me feel trapped," he said, surprised as the words came out. "Not in the same way as the dungeon of Carrion Tomb. It's different. I just don't want to disappoint anybody."

"That's the tension that sits on your shoulders. And flows through your body. And it will be sensed by Palojax or any other wise creature of the wood or mountain or lake."

Wily was getting very uncomfortable. It felt like Olgara's words were digging into him like a burrowing tick trying to find blood. "None of this is helping me learn how to quell," he snapped. "You told my mother and uncle and I that I needed to use pressure points to calm the lair beast."

"You need to press at the top of the back on either side of the spine," Olgara continued, "But the spots where you press are not nearly as important as the energy that flows through your fingers. You need to release all that pressure you put on yourself before you ever touch a lair beast."

Wily thought that sounded ridiculous. *When I used to calm the crab dragons, they didn't care how I was feeling. They didn't care that I had been miserable living in a dungeon my whole life. How does any of this matter?*

"Here's what you must understand," Olgara said slowly. "You don't need to be perfect. You can't get everything right. In fact, most things you will get wrong. And that's okay. That's part of life."

Wily nodded at her words, but inside he knew that she had no idea what it was like to be a prince of

Panthasos. She had spent all of her life out here in the wild, with far fewer responsibilities. She couldn't possibly know how he felt.

"I understand," Wily said, trying to placate her.

Olgara looked at him as if she didn't quite believe him.

"Stalag is building his army of stone golems," Wily said, "and it's growing with every hour we do nothing."

"I see your shoulders rising again."

Wily was getting frustrated. "Of course they are," he snapped. "Haven't you been listening to what I've been saying?"

"I've been listening very carefully," she said. "Have you?"

Olgara turned around and headed down the curved trunk of the tree.

"No more lessons," she said with a long sigh. "I will point you back to the Roamabout camp. I can help you no more."

oOo

WHEN WILY GOT back to the camp, he found that while the elder members of the tribe continued to keep their distance, the younger Roamabouts had warmed to his companions. Moshul was sitting in the middle of a group of toddlers who, along with their animal friends, were using him like a giant climbing structure. Bunny rabbits bounded across the moss golem's legs, and mice crawled through his toes. Moshul seemed delighted by all the attention.

Righteous was arm wrestling some of the burlier teenagers of the tribe and chalking up victories. Wily watched as one Roamabout, nearly the size of a small bear, took a seat on the ground opposite Righteous and locked hands with the magical arm. Within seconds the teenager's face was flushed red. He was struggling with all his might, but to no avail: he let out a groan as Righteous pinned his hand to the log.

Odette and Roveeka were playing a very messy game with another group of kids. A large circle had been set up and everyone paired off in teams of two. One member of each team stood in the circle with their eyes blindfolded and hands coated with thick, sticky honey. When each round began, a rock beetle would be released in the center of the circle. It would buzz around as the blindfolded, honey-handed teammates tried to catch it. Of course, without being able to see, the only way they even had a chance to snag a flying beetle was to listen to the shouted directions of their other team member who sat on the ground near the circle. After watching just one round, Wily could tell that the real fun of the game was when the team members in the circle collided and gave each other a face full of sticky honey.

"You did that on purpose!" Odette shouted as honey dripped down her shirt and lips.

"May-be," Roveeka said with a sly grin.

All the kids burst into a fit of giggles, even Odette, who was wiping the sticky goo from her cheeks and licking it.

*They're so happy,* Wily thought as he looked at Roveeka and Odette. *But that will change as soon as they discover I barely learned a thing from Olgara.*

"How'd it go?" Pryvyd called out.

Wily turned to see the knight sitting with Lumina and Talleywin near a large tree. His mother, her injured leg wrapped in bandages, looked up at him with so much hope. She would be so disappointed once she learned the truth. If only there were some other way to quell the lair beast. He looked across the clearing to the quiet stream where Valor was lounging with her mountain lion. For a moment, Wily considered begging her, but he had a very strong feeling that would only make her want to help him less. Wily turned back to Pryvyd, his mother, and his uncle.

"It went great," Wily lied. "Olgara was surprised by how fast I got the hang of it."

Both Lumina and Pryvyd beamed.

"Olgara thinks that I should go practice on the manticorn once before heading off to the Below," Wily continued. "She said that Valor should take me to find it."

"That's fantastic news," Lumina said, getting slowly to her feet.

"I could take you," Talleywin said. "Valor won't be keen to help."

"No," Wily said curtly. "Olgara said it had to be her."

"Very well," he said. "She's wiser than me."

Talleywin led Wily to where Valor was sitting with Stalkeer. "Valor," Talleywin said, "can we speak with you for a minute?"

Stalkeer growled at him.

"For a minute," Valor said, calming her feline companion.

"Wily needs to be taken to the High Wing Pool to practice quelling the manticorn."

"Find someone else," Valor said. "I don't feel like watching him getting eaten."

"Olgara asked that you do it," Talleywin said.

"She did," Wily lied again. "It was a very specific request."

Valor stared at Wily with skeptical eyes. After a moment, her demeanor changed. "If it's really what Olgara wanted," she said, quickly leaping to her feet. "We leave now. I don't want to miss dinner."

oOo

VALOR MOVED QUICKLY through the woods, not seeming to mind that Wily was tripping over roots and fallen branches as he tried to keep pace.

"You don't seem to have a lot of experience with this," Valor said. "It's called walking. Most Roamabouts learn how to do it when they're toddlers."

"I bet you wouldn't be quite as swift in a dungeon," Wily retorted.

"Left. Right. Left. Right. I think walking is pretty much the same everywhere."

Valor and Wily left the woods at the base of one of the legs of Spider Rock. As impressive as it had looked from a distance, here, at its foot, it was positively imposing. A path wound its way beneath three of the legs of the stone spider alongside the cliff wall of the Web.

As they passed under the second leg of Spider Rock, Wily had to stop for a moment to catch his breath.

"Tired already?" Valor asked. "Must be from too much time eating cookies in the dining room and not enough time out in the wild exercising."

"It's the thin mountain air," Wily countered. "I'm still used to thick cave air."

"Tell yourself whatever you want," Valor said. "But the air up here is just as easy to breathe as anywhere else."

Wily took a gulp of air and wondered if she was right.

"I thought a king was supposed to make decisions. Not excuses."

"That wasn't an excuse. I just got tired for a moment."

"And there's excuse number two. For someone who's supposedly going to be keeping Panthasos safe, you don't inspire a lot of confidence."

"Sitting on the throne is not an easy job," Wily said.

"I bet you do the sitting part just fine. It's everything else you probably have trouble with."

Wily wanted to snap back but he knew right now was

not the moment. He still needed her help. A lot of her help.

As they continued higher, the dirt path slowly faded into a scramble of wobbly rocks that shook as they were stepped on.

"Make sure you watch where you put your feet," Valor called back. "The cuttlestones can give quite a sting if you stomp on their backs."

"What's a cuttlestone?" Wily asked as he looked down at the rough terrain.

"It's kind of like a land squid," Valor explained, "with a stinger as long as your thumb, filled with a toxin that causes intense itching that lasts for a whole year."

"What do they look like?" Wily asked with growing fear.

"Round stones with black speckles."

Wily looked down at the ground and froze in place. "But all the rocks are round with black speckles!"

"You're right," Valor said with a wicked smile. "You should have worn a pair of shoes with thicker soles."

Wily took cautious steps forward, giving each rock a small nudge before stepping on it. Valor seemed to be enjoying this a little too much.

As they moved higher up the Web, the rocks changed over to boulders that required scrambling up and over. Wily could tell that Valor was surprised by his climbing skills. He was used to clinging to much more precarious surfaces. Climbing boulders was much easier than scaling a greased wall over a boiling lava pit. But Valor was not eager to give out compliments.

After a short stretch of boulders, the mountain leveled out into a field of tall grass. Crickets and tumble-bugs scurried past Wily's ankles toward a wall of reeds ahead. As they got closer, frogs and slynx peeked their heads above the thick weeds to catch a glimpse of the unusual human visitors.

"Animals from mountains away travel here to drink from the High Wing Pool," Valor said as she lightened her steps. "The water can heal wounds with a few drinks and fill you with the strength of a beast three times your own size. It's even rumored to make you grow larger if you drink enough of it." Valor took measure of Wily. "Maybe you should get a couple jugs yourself."

"Hey!" Wily said, offended. "I'm average height."

"Maybe for a gwarf or a squatling."

Wily lifted his shoulders high to make himself an inch or two taller. "I'm still growing," he said defiantly.

As Valor pushed aside the first reeds, she turned back to Wily and whispered, "I don't know what we might see in there. So just stay calm."

She moved quietly through the dense reeds. Wily was less stealthy, his knees knocking the long shoots. Ahead, Wily saw a sparkling blue pool with a dozen animals gathered around it. Back when he first exited Carrion Tomb, he might have been terrified by the tall herons standing knee deep in the water, but that was before he realized that most birds were completely harmless. "I'm guessing none of these creatures are the manticorn," he said, eyeing mountain mice and a sleeping sloth.

Valor circled around to a patch of unoccupied mud on the far side of the pool. She bent down near it. "I think we might have just missed it," she said excitedly. "The print is still fresh."

Valor turned to one of the herons standing in the pool. Its long beak poked the water, searching for tadpoles. Valor cupped her hands over her mouth and began making low cawing sounds.

After a moment, the heron replied with a series of whistles and caws. Wily was skilled in Grunt, Arachnid, and Gargletongue, but the language of birds was completely foreign to him.

"The manticorn left just moments ago," Valor explained to Wily. "Maybe even as we were pushing through the reeds. It must have sensed us coming. They're not keen on any two-legged creature." She gestured to the reeds. "If we hurry, we may be able to catch up with it."

Before following her, Wily dropped to his knees beside the pool and pulled a vial from his pouch. While Valor wasn't watching, Wily uncorked the vial and scooped it into the pool, filling it. He wouldn't mind growing a couple extra inches, but Valor didn't need to know that. He slipped the vial back into his trapsmith belt. Then, splashing past the snoring sloth splayed out on the mud, he hurried after Valor, who was fast disappearing into the reeds.

## 10

# THE MANTICORN

As Valor led them out of the reeds, Wily found himself on one of the jutting precipices of the Web. The view to the forest below was staggering, and looking far to the north, Wily thought he could spot the lake that was home to the Floating City and the mountains beyond that hid the entrance to Carrion Tomb. But Wily knew his attention should be on the nearby cave and the strange pattern of claw prints in the mud in front of it.

"Do you think it's inside?" Wily asked as he peered into the darkness of the cave.

"Nope," Valor said. "I think it's right behind you."

Wily turned to see a two-headed beast crawling toward him on six clawed legs. It had the body and tail of a giant panther—but its two heads were not a panther's. One head resembled an eagle with a giant horn sticking out from between its eyes. The other looked as if it had been taken from a goat, except that it had dagger-sharp fangs where its teeth should be. Neither head looked friendly.

"I'd say good luck," Valor said as she scurried over and took cover behind a nearby rock, "but I think you're going to need a lot more than that."

Wily's heart was racing as he faced the beast on his own. The manticorn didn't hesitate. It pounced on Wily, its mighty body striking the ground just as he rolled away. The eagle head let out an ear-piercing screech. Not to be outdone, the goat released a terrifying bleat.

*I've faced off against crab dragons and fed swarms of ghost spiders without blinking an eye,* Wily reassured himself. *Just take it nice and easy.*

He reached into his pouch and pulled out a slice of tunnel trout. Both heads of the manticorn eyed the salted fish in his hand.

"That's right," Wily said, holding the fish out before him. "Salted tunnel trout. Very yummy."

The two heads of the manticorn snapped the air as it moved closer.

"Which of you is going to get it?" Wily asked.

As both heads lunged for the briny treat, Wily took a quick step back and tossed the fish over the manticorn. The salty treat landed behind the beast.

Unfortunately, the beast didn't turn for it the way a giant scorpion or ghost spider would have. It kept all four of its eyes locked on Wily and let out another screech and bleat in unison. And although Wily was not fluent in either Avian or Hoofspeak, he was pretty sure the manticorn's two heads had said something to the effect of "I'm not falling for that. I've got my eyes on a bigger meal." The manticorn pounced again at Wily, who scrambled back and grabbed a tree branch to defend himself.

He was cornered.

*This is it,* Wily thought. *This is the moment when Valor will see that I'm in mortal danger, come rescue me, quell the manticorn, and change her mind about helping us on our quest.*

He looked over his shoulder to find—that Valor was nowhere to be seen.

The manticorn moved closer, preparing to feast.

*This is not what I expected to happen,* Wily thought. "Valor!" he called out. "I need help!"

"If Olgara thought you were ready," Valor replied from her hiding spot, "I'm sure you've got this."

Wily realized he had to do this on his own. *I need to find a way to get on the back of the manticorn and quell it myself.*

Wily knew what Odette would do if she were in this situation: she'd use the stick he was holding to vault up and over the two manticorn heads, making a perfect landing on the beast's back. The problem was that he was not trained to pull off that complicated an acrobatic maneuver. Besides, backflips were not the way he dealt with trouble. He invented his way out of problems. He scanned the ground for a solution. *Is there something I could use as springs for my shoes? Or a giant elastic string to launch myself like a tomato from a slingshot?*

As he dodged the sharp horn jutting out of the eagle's forehead, he spotted an oval-shaped rock on the ground. Then he looked down at the branch in his hand. He could use it to make a simple lever, just a beam and a fulcrum.

Now the ram's head lunged at Wily with its black-tipped fangs. He rolled out of the way and laid the branch on top of the rock so that it was perfectly balanced in the center. Wily hopped onto the end of the branch that was closer to the manticorn, then turned to face the beast as it stalked forward.

"Okay!" Wily taunted the beast. "Pounce on me."

The manticorn bent its knees just like it had before, preparing to leap. As it launched itself into the air, Wily quickly backed up, positioning himself on the other side of the makeshift seesaw. When the manticorn landed on the empty, elevated side of the lever, the impact sent Wily flying into the air, up and over the heads of the beast. Wily landed on the back of the manticorn, facing the creature's tail.

As the manticorn tried to buck Wily to the ground, he slid up its back and spun around so that he was facing the front of the thrashing beast. He found the spot at the base of the two necks and grabbed it with his fingers.

*I can do this,* Wily thought. *Quell the manticorn.*

He squeezed tightly down on the spot where the eagle and goat necks joined together.

*Use calm energy. Channel it into the pressure point.*

The manticorn lashed wildly, kicking its hind legs.

*You have to do this right,* Wily silently shouted at himself. *Everyone is counting on you.*

It wasn't working. The beast was beginning to thrash more.

*What am I doing wrong?*

He had the sudden feeling that he was going to disappoint all his friends. All the people of Panthasos who were counting on him to be perfect. The pressure he'd been feeling over the last few months pressed down on his shoulders heavier than ever before.

The manticorn was only getting more riled. Wily realized he was channeling the wrong kind of energy. But the panic of doing the wrong thing only got him more agitated.

*I can't quell the beast. I can't do any of this. It's too hard to be the perfect prince. The perfect future king. It's all too much.*

The manticorn shook its back with such force that Wily went flying into a boulder on the edge of the Web's jagged cliff. All the air went out of him, and when he was finally able to breathe again and looked up, the manticorn was practically on top of him.

Then, from the corner of his eye, he saw Valor running. She let out a wild bird screech that sent a flock of herons fluttering out of the bushes. The manticorn was distracted by the birds. It snatched one with its beaked eagle mouth.

This gave Valor enough time to jump onto the manticorn's back. Wily watched as the manticorn tried to shake her. But as the beast struggled, it seemed to be slowly losing the will to fight.

"Down!" Valor said as she pressed her hands firmly into the beast's neck.

The manticorn dropped its belly to the ground submissively. Then it opened its mouth and let the caught heron limp away with only an injured wing.

After another moment, the manticorn's two heads began to coo and baa quietly.

Valor bounded off the back of the creature. "Who's a good two-headed manticorn?" she said as she scratched behind the goat head's ear.

The eagle head gently nudged Valor's shoulder with its horn.

"I haven't forgotten about you," Valor said. She gently stroked the line of white feathers above the eagle head's eyes.

The manticorn rolled over, exposing its furry belly. Valor kneeled down to give it some soft belly rubs.

Then Valor turned to Wily. "I knew what you were planning from the moment we left," she said. "I saw right through your lie. Olgara would never have asked me to take you. You thought that you could turn me into the hero. Make me see myself in a new light. And that I would join you on your mission."

"Well . . . ," Wily said, "will you?"

"Not a chance. I don't need to be a hero for Panthasos. Let the kingdom fall for all I care."

"Then why did you bring me up here?" Wily asked.

"Because it was fun watching you squirm."

"You came just to *embarrass* me?" Wily said, feeling his cheeks redden.

"You're going to need to find another way to deal with the stone golems," Valor continued. "Because there's no way you are quelling a lair beast. Maybe you could get a chisel and chip away at them very slowly."

Valor turned and started back through the reeds with the manticorn following behind, tail wagging happily.

Wily wondered what he was going to do. If the pressure of princehood had seemed heavy before, now it felt as if he were a single stone pillar supporting an entire mountain range.

oᎾo

DURING THEIR WALK back down the mountain, Wily had tried several times to appeal to Valor's sympathy. He hadn't been doing a very good job.

"The Roamabouts don't need towns or villages or castles," Valor said. "They only create more problems. The stone golems will be doing us all a favor."

"Stalag and his fellow mages," Wily pleaded, "care only about themselves. They'll use the throne to fill their own vaults while the less fortunate suffer."

"Doesn't sound like my problem," Valor said. "Or the problem of any of the wild beasts of the land."

Both heads of the manticorn snorted in agreement.

As the path twisted under the stone legs of Spider Rock, Wily wondered how he was going to break the horrible news to the others. He had failed them and every Panthasan who Stalag would soon treat with the same cruelty he had shown Wily for all those years in Carrion Tomb.

Just ahead, Valor raised a hand to signal Wily and the manticorn to stop. She bent down near a small mushroom patch.

"Is it dangerous?" Wily called out cautiously.

"Not in the least," she replied. "I just don't want you scaring it away."

Valor reached out and picked up something gently in her hands. Wily moved closer and saw she was holding a small furry animal with eyes that took up half its face.

"What is it?" Wily asked.

"A baby wildeboar," Valor said. "He must have wandered off." She spoke directly to the wildeboar. "Your mother must be terrified. You need to stay near her until you grow your first pair of tusks."

The small little animal gave a timid squeak. Then it nuzzled tightly into Valor's hands, pressing its snout into the crook of her thumb and forefinger.

"You are a cute one," she said with a smile.

The manticorn's two heads bleated and squawked in unison.

"You're very cute too," Valor reassured the manticorn.

Both the eagle head and goat head seemed to grin, satisfied.

"You stay here," Valor gently commanded the manticorn.

The beast lay down, pressing its body up against the warm, dusty road. Wily was impressed. Even the beasts of Carrion Tomb that he'd spent his entire life training had never responded with such understanding and obedience.

Valor stepped off the path and into the underbrush. Wily followed behind her as she stepped over berry shrubs and chunks of rock that must have slid down the steep cliff during the last rainstorm.

"Shhhh," Valor admonished him. "We don't want to scare away the rest of the family."

Wily could have sworn he was being just as silent as her, but clearly she would have disagreed.

"Many small animals make their homes here because

of the safety it provides. The arches of Spider Rock block the view of the terrorhawks that patrol the clouds. And the hunters from the neighboring villages stay away in fear of the bigger beasts that lurk in the forest."

As they approached the rocky mountainside, the wildeboar sniffed the air and gave a little squeal of happiness. The underside of Spider Rock was teeming with life. Families of swallows had built mud nests all along the cracks in the stone. Frogs and lizards bathed in the small pools made from the dripping rocks above. Mice and ferrets stuck their heads out from the burrows in the dirt. From the path just a few strides away, none of this could be seen. Wily was amazed by how much life was hidden just beyond his eyes. It reminded him of the maintenance tunnels of Carrion Tomb; while most invaders saw only the main path, there was so much secretly happening just out of sight.

"Look," Valor said with a grin, "there's his family."

Wily spied a mama wildeboar with her squeal of pups gathered around her. The mama boar began to grunt as Valor approached with the baby in hand. She gently put it down on the ground. The baby wildeboar ran to its mother's side, happily joining its siblings. The mother wildeboar gave a little squeal to Valor, thanking her.

The sweet reunion gave Wily a comforting rush of good feelings. It almost made him forget all about what had just happened with the manticorn.

"I care about the people of Panthasos the way you

care about these animals," Wily said. "Please help me. If you just met some of the wall-dwellers, I think—"

"You think you have something to teach me?" Valor scoffed. "The boy who spent his whole life underground? You're the one that's sheltered. You're the one who has a lot to learn."

"In the last few months, I've grown so much."

"Don't make me laugh," Valor said as she clenched her fist. "I saw what your father did. What a king is capable of. You will be no different from him. And this Stalag you talk about will be no different either. No person should rule anyone else. Especially if they're only twelve."

Valor turned her back on Wily and stormed away, leaving him with the menagerie of animals. The birds, mammals, and reptiles all stared at him.

*Valor's right,* he thought bitterly. He might be the future king of Panthasos, but the last thing these animals needed was somebody to rule over them.

## 11

# SPIDER CRACKING

For the rest of the walk downhill, Wily was left thinking about how he'd break the bad news to his companions. There was no version that sounded quite right. *Hey, everyone, I lied about being able to train the manticorn, and there's no way I could even come close to quelling the ancient lair beast. And by the way, Valor, our only hope, hates me more than ever.* He knew that his mother would be especially disappointed. She had put so much faith in him.

By the time they reached the bottom of the Web, the waxing moon was high in the sky and the stars twinkled like drops of water dangling from the fine threads of a ghost spider's web. Valor led the way, but Wily would have only needed to follow the scent of baked blackberry crumble to find his way back to the Roamabout camp. As Valor, Wily, and the quelled manticorn made their way out of the woods and into the clearing, every member of the Roamabouts looked up from their dessert.

"A manticorn!" a burly Roamabout shouted. "It's been quelled."

Roveeka dropped her piece of crumble and bounded up from the wooden log she'd been sitting on. She ran for Wily as fast as her uneven legs would carry her and embraced him in a big hug. "You did it!" Roveeka exclaimed, eyeing the manticorn. "Was it very difficult? I want to hear the whole story!"

Everyone looked at Wily.

"I didn't do anything," Wily said. "Except nearly get eaten. Valor tamed the manticorn."

The entire crowd turned their attention to Valor. A chorus of congratulations and cheers followed. As Valor and the manticorn made their way to the fires in the middle of camp, Wily was left alone. With a forlorn expression, he wandered over to an isolated rock and took a seat.

"Can I join you for a moment?"

He looked up to see his mother limping toward him.

"I lied to you about what Olgara said," Wily told his mom. "I can't quell Palojax. I thought I could convince Valor to come with us. But I didn't do a good job at that either. How will I ever be able to lead all of Panthasos?"

"Don't be so hard on yourself," Lumina said.

"Everyone is counting on me," Wily said. "We have to defeat Stalag."

"You've got to remember that you are only a person," Lumina said. "Sometimes you'll succeed. And sometimes you'll fail. And both are okay."

"I can't fail," Wily said. "If I fail, the kingdom will be overrun by an army of stone golems."

"Everyone fails," Lumina said. "Not only sometimes. But most of the time. This is how we grow. This is how we learn."

Wily nodded his head, but his mother's words didn't offer much comfort.

"Let me go talk with Valor," she said.

"I already asked her to help," Wily said. "She wasn't interested."

"I'll try again. And if she refuses . . . we'll figure it out." Lumina gave Wily a kiss on his forehead and slowly walked toward the crowd of laughing and singing Roamabouts gathered around Valor.

Wily watched as Lumina gently pulled Valor out of the crowd. From this distance, Wily couldn't hear what she was saying, but he could see Valor's face slowly turn to a grimace. Valor began to shake her head vehemently. Lumina tried to take her hand but Valor knocked it away. Lumina kept talking, but all Wily could hear was the boisterous chanting of the celebrating Roamabouts.

Then suddenly, Valor raised her voice. "I don't want to help you!" she yelled. "Just leave me alone. This is not my problem."

With that, Valor stormed away from Lumina and took a seat in the grass next to Stalkeer.

Just then, the forest floor began to rumble. For a moment, Wily wondered if the monsoonodon had returned. Then he turned in the direction of the sound.

The cliffs of the Web were crumbling. Rocks were breaking off the sheer surface and tumbling to the ground, smacking against the stone pillars that held up Spider Rock.

"On the mountaintop," Odette said, pointing to the peaks of the Web where Wily had just been.

There, in silhouette against the darkened sky, a dozen stone golems marched to the west. Their massive weight was toppling the boulders that lay just beyond the High Wing Pools. Wily watched in horror as a splintering crack formed down a leg of Spider Rock. As the stone golems continued to move along the peaks of the Web, one of the spider legs snapped off completely and went tumbling to the ground.

Everybody leaped to their feet, looking up at the mountain with horror. Wily heard Valor shout, "The animals!" followed by, "Stalkeer!"

The black-and-gold mountain lion bounded over to her, and Valor pulled herself onto her mount's back.

"No," Lumina said, limping into Valor's path. "It's too dangerous."

"You don't have any business telling me what I can

or can't do," Valor said, urging Stalkeer to move around Lumina.

In the distance, a second spider leg was fracturing under the increasing pressure.

"I may have been away," Lumina said, "but I'm still someone who cares about you. Get off that mountain lion."

"You lost the privilege to tell me what to do when you abandoned me, Auntie," Valor said.

"Then listen to *me*," Talleywin said, moving next to Lumina and further blocking Stalkeer's path to the Web.

"I've got to protect my pack," Valor added.

As another loud crack echoed over the hillside, Valor gave Stalkeer a firm pat on the side of her neck. Effortlessly, the mountain lion leaped over both Talleywin's and Lumina's heads and bounded toward the tree line.

As Wily watched her go, he imagined the little wildeboar and its family huddling together in fear. He could picture in his head all the animals under Spider Rock that were in terrible danger. *Will they get away in time, or will they all be crushed when Spider Rock falls from its high perch?*

Wily spied Odette's horse grazing nearby and called out to his elf companion. "I need to borrow your horse."

"Not without me on the back of it," Odette replied as she whistled loudly.

Odette mounted her horse in her usual manner: with

a single handspring leap from behind, vaulting herself over the tail and sliding across the mare's back until her fingers were clutching the mane. She reached down a hand for Wily and pulled him onto the horse.

"No, Wily!" Lumina said as she stepped in front of Odette's horse.

"Mom, I've got to help the animals," Wily said.

"I absolutely prohibit it."

"It's the right thing to do."

She gave him a hard, long look, then sighed and stepped aside to allow them to pass. Odette gave a quick heel to her horse's side and the mount took off in pursuit of Stalkeer and Valor.

"I'll keep an eye on him," Odette called back to Lumina.

As Odette's horse galloped through the dark mesh of trees, Wily could see the great stone body of the spider was beginning to wobble on its six remaining legs. The shift in weight appeared to have destabilized the towering structure. A third leg, covered with vines and shade moss, was cracking like a wooden shield in the claw of a crab dragon.

"These better be some very cute animals we're saving," Odette said. "Not just toads and lizards."

As the horse approached the vine-covered leg, the top of the spider's stone pedestal began to give way. With a crack, a huge block of stone snapped off the leg. It came smashing down, snapping tree branches and sending birds into flight. The stone block hit the earth only a dozen feet in front of Odette's horse. The animal reared up in terror.

"Come on, girl." Odette tried to urge her on.

But the horse refused to go any farther. Ahead, Wily could see Valor running out from under Spider Rock with an armful of baby raccoons. Stalkeer bounded beside her with the mother raccoon held gently in her jaws. Within seconds they reached Wily and Odette, rushed past them, and put the woodland creatures down in the safety of the underbrush.

"Are you just going to sit there or are you going to help?" Valor called out to Wily and Odette as she raced back toward the mountain.

Odette and Wily slid off the horse and charged past the crumbling pedestal of rock. Wily hurried to the spot where Valor had reunited the baby wildeboar with its mother. He could see the animals weren't fleeing but instead wedging themselves deeper into the cracks in the rocks.

"If Spider Rock comes down," Valor shouted to Wily, "they'll all be buried under here."

"If Spider Rock comes down," Odette added, "we will be too."

"Caroo," Valor called up to a cluster of birds peeking their trembling heads from mud nests built into crevices of the vine-covered leg of Spider Rock. "Caroo."

Although hesitant, the birds heeded her warning and

took flight, leaving their protective shelters. It wasn't a moment too soon either: moments later, the pillar of stone came crashing down, hitting the mountainside.

"All the legs are starting to fall!" Valor screamed. "Take as many animals as you can and run."

Odette beckoned to a group of tiny mice. Before she could even scoop them up, a whole pack of terrified toads bounced up to her and started hopping in her pockets and pouches. She grabbed as many mice as she could and ran away from the wall.

Valor, meanwhile, was pulling frightened hedgehogs out of a rotted log, and Wily was squatting in front of a dozen tarantulas.

"Get on my arm," Wily pleaded in Arachnid.

The bristly spiders scurried up his forearm, their sharp feet digging into his skin. The twelve formed a line along the long burn mark that stretched from Wily's wrist to elbow.

Just then, a giant rock came crashing down the slope. It would have struck Wily on the head if Valor hadn't pushed him clear in the nick of time.

Wily turned to run and expected Valor to be at his side. Instead he saw she was heading back into danger with the hedgehogs tucked in the crook of her arm. She had stopped in front of a hole in the ground. Wily could see the same young wildeboar that had gotten lost from its mother peeking out. Above, all of Spider Rock was starting to topple.

"Come on!" Wily cried.

"I won't leave him behind," Valor said, reaching into the hole.

"You have to," Wily shouted back.

As another chunk of rock came falling, Wily could see Valor was torn. The wildeboar was still out of reach. All around them, Wily could hear the sound of shattering stone. Spider Rock was coming down.

Valor turned away from the hole and sprinted away with the hedgehogs. Wily could see tears streaming across her cheeks. They both made for the relative safety of the tree line, but before they reached it, the bulbous body of the great spider fell, and fell, and fell—and hit the ground. The impact knocked Wily off his feet, sending him rolling forward. The tarantulas scattered into the underbrush as Wily bounced to a stop beside Valor.

When he looked back, he saw that what had once been a safe place for all animals was now nothing more than a pile of crushed rocks. Valor looked back sadly at the desolation.

"If we don't find a way to stop the stone golems, this is only the beginning," Wily said. "Stalag's army will only grow in power."

Valor nodded.

"I will join you to find Palojax," she said after a long silence. "Not to help *you*. Or your mother. Or the people of Panthasos. I will join you to help the *animals,* the creatures that will be hurt most in this battle of which they have no part."

"Thank you," Wily said. "You will not regret it."

Valor gave him a cold stare. "Don't thank me. I might still change my mind."

# THE ORACLE OF OAK

The next morning, as Wily and the others were preparing to leave, his mother limped to his side, wincing with each step.

"I need go back to the palace," Lumina said. "My leg is only getting worse. I can't slow you down."

"You won't," Wily said.

"We both know I will," she replied. "Besides, somebody has to make sure the royal palace will remain standing until you return with Palojax." Lumina touched Wily's cheek softly with her hand. Then she turned to the others who were preparing their mounts. "The only sage within a day's travel is the Oracle of Oak," she said. "She will know how to get into the Below. That's where you should head next. Do you know where to find her?"

"Rootmire Glen," Odette said with a nod. "We've

visited her before. She guided us to a very important person."

Which was absolutely true: it had been the Oracle of Oak who had told Odette, Moshul, and Pryvyd to seek the trapsmith of Carrion Tomb. If it hadn't been for her, Wily might still be polishing the gears of the snap traps and feeding the ghost spiders in the subterranean tunnels of Stalag's dungeon.

"That's to the north," Valor said. "The same direction the golems on the Web were heading."

"Then we'll have to proceed with caution," Pryvyd said.

"And here are the jewels you should give to the oracle as payment." Lumina handed a leather bag to Pryvyd. Then she called over to Impish and Gremlin. "Come on, you two. Say your good-byes."

The two ferrets bounded down Moshul's partially flattened back to the ground. They scampered over to Lumina and scurried up into her jacket pockets, tucking themselves in comfortably for the long ride ahead.

Then it was time for Lumina to say good-bye to her son. She enfolded Wily in a big embrace.

He whispered in her ear, "I wish you could come with us."

"You did just fine without me before," Lumina replied quietly. "You'll do just fine now too."

She let go of Wily and glanced over at the others. "Take care of him," Lumina said.

"A future king who needs to be watched over?" Valor scoffed. "That's reassuring."

Wily felt his cheeks flush red as his mother mounted her horse. She gave a final wave to the companions and rode away.

Valor didn't even wait for Lumina to disappear into the trees before turning to the others. "If we want to reach Rootmire Glen without being spotted by the golems," she explained, "we should cut through the Opake Woods."

Odette was used to being the alpha-female, the leader of the band. Her humorless expression indicated she wasn't happy to have to relinquish her role.

"Why don't you lead the way?" Pryvyd said to Valor as he mounted his horse.

"I was planning to," Valor said. "Follow me. And try to keep up."

With one swift movement, she was on Stalkeer's back. The mountain lion roared with delight and bounded ahead.

oOo

THE OPAKE WOODS were different than the other forests Wily had traveled through. The leaves of the noxen trees that populated the woods were coal black. Even during daytime, the forest was as dim as a torch-lit tunnel. Valor was only three horse-lengths ahead of him, but to Wily she was nearly enveloped in darkness.

"A golem!" a voice that sounded like Pryvyd's shouted from behind.

Wily spun around in a panic. *A golem, here? Even in the dark shade of the Opake Woods? Was there nowhere they hadn't reached?*

"I don't see any golems," Roveeka called out from Moshul's shoulders. "Where is it, Pryvyd?"

Roveeka could see as well in the dark as she could in the light. *How did she not see it?*

"I didn't say anything," Pryvyd yelled. "That was someone else."

"Bring it down!" the same voice from the trees called out.

Suddenly, a spear flew from the trees and landed at Moshul's feet.

"I know where the golem is," Odette called back to Roveeka. "Beneath your legs."

The strangers in the trees were talking about Moshul. A dozen spears flew from the foliage toward the moss golem and his friends. Pryvyd blocked one with his shield while Righteous plucked another from the air. Moshul was struck with four in his chest and a fifth in his arm. The moss golem stumbled backward, causing Roveeka to lose her balance. She grabbed a fistful of shoulder mushrooms to steady herself.

"I can't hold on," Roveeka said as the fungus was torn from the soil on Moshul's back.

She tipped from her perch and went tumbling toward

the ground. Before she hit the earth, Stalkeer and Valor jumped underneath the falling hobgoblet. After catching Roveeka, they dodged a barrage of arrows from the thick shrubs.

"Glad someone around here can act under pressure," Valor snapped, eyeing Wily with exasperation.

"Keep firing," the voice yelled. "We've got them pinned down."

An arrow whizzed past Wily, scraping his earlobe. Another arrow struck a pouch on his tool belt; just a few inches higher and it would have been sticking out of his belly.

"I recognize that voice," Pryvyd said. He raised his hand and threw down his shield. "I am Pryvyd Rucka, Knight of the Golden Sun."

The arrows stopped. Odette and Wily exchanged nervous glances.

"Are you a prisoner of the stone golem?" a new voice in the bushes called back.

"This is not a stone golem," Pryvyd yelled. "He is just moss and mud and my friend."

A stout woman with a close-cropped head of curly hair walked out from the dense brush. Her armor, while cracked and dented, was unmistakable. It bore the same insignia as Pryvyd's.

"Well if isn't the most noble warrior in all the land," she said with a smile. "Get over here, Righteous."

Righteous flew to the woman's side and the two gave

each other a complicated handshake that involved finger slaps and fist bumps. The woman then looked over at Pryvyd. "You're still following your arm around?" she asked. "I thought you'd be sleeping in an alley outside Ratgull Harbor by now."

"Nice to see you too, Spraved," Pryvyd said without cracking a smile.

"These woods used to be filled with thieves, so you should feel right at home," Spraved said, spitting on the ground.

"I made a mistake," Pryvyd said. "I'm a knight again."

"Once a thief, always a thief," Spraved replied. "You left when we needed you most. You stole hope from us. That is not so easily returned."

A squad of knights emerged from the dense leaves. All of them looked like they'd been through some tough fights.

"I am joined by Wily Snare, heir to the throne," Pryvyd said. "We're on our way to Rootmire Glen."

"It's very dangerous to head in that direction," Spraved muttered. "Everything north of here has become golem territory. From the glen all the way past Frenig Volcano."

"What about Halberd Keep?" Pryvyd asked, his voice rising with concern.

"It's in bad shape," Spraved said. "A pack of golems blitzed it in the middle of the night. They tore down the outer walls before we could run them off. We've been ambushing golems here, hoping to give the other soldiers a chance to rebuild before the next attack."

"We have to reach the Oracle of Oak," Wily insisted. "The safety of all Panthasos is depending on it."

"Then we will take you," she said. "Despite your company."

Spraved approached Moshul and looked up at him. "Sorry about the spears," she said. "It's hard to see very far in these dark woods." Then she gave Moshul another hard stare. "And it looks like I might have missed an incredible sight. You're beautiful. Someone had a real eye when they put you together."

Moshul looked surprised. He signed something to Odette.

"He says that he is a mistake," Odette said. "Unfinished."

"He doesn't look like a mistake to me," Spraved said.

Moshul signed again, and Odette translated. "He says he doesn't even have a mouth."

"And it doesn't look like you need a mouth to speak," Spraved replied. "Perhaps you can say more without a mouth than you would have ever said with one."

Moshul dropped his hands to his sides. He appeared to be at a loss for words. Even more so than normal.

○◯○

As the group moved north through the woods, Spraved's soldiers kept a tight circle around the travelers, as if the trees themselves could attack at any moment. They were on high alert; even the slightest noise was reason enough to raise their spears in defense.

By the time they exited Opake, Wily was surprised to find it was already late in the afternoon. The sun was setting to the west, coloring the clouds a deep orange and pink. Since the very first sunset Wily had seen, he had been amazed by the seemingly magical ability of nature to change the color of the sky. But it wasn't just the sky that looked amazing; the rolling hills in the distance were covered with a bewildering tangle of twisting blue lines that crisscrossed and overlapped.

"What are those?" Roveeka asked from high atop Moshul's shoulders. "Sleeping snakes?"

"The roots of the Great Blue Oak," Odette said. "They all lead back to a single tree. That's where the oracle sits, watching the world."

"They say the roots stretch beyond these hills as well," Pryvyd added. "Twisting below the surface of the earth to every corner of Panthasos. That's how the tree and the oracle know so much."

"A tree is just a plant," Wily said. "How can it know anything?"

Valor chimed in from ahead. "Sometimes a tree can be brilliant and a person can be a fool."

"I'm not a fool," he said.

"All men and women who sit on chairs and think that it brings them power are fools," Valor replied. "And you might be the biggest one of all. I heard someone mention that you're afraid of butterflies. Is it their big teeth that scare you? Or their claws?"

"I was afraid at first," Wily responded. "But that's just because I didn't know any better."

"So what changed?" Valor taunted.

It was almost completely dark when the companions and the soldiers of Halberd Keep reached the first of the twisting blue roots. They followed them all the way to a glen with an enormous blue-barked oak tree growing in its middle. The tree's leaves were an even brighter hue than its roots; they matched the color of Odette's eyes.

A small woman sat cross-legged on a solid mesh of roots that was so tightly packed, it appeared to be a bumpy wooden floor. Her long, gray-blue hair snaked down her shoulders like the roots curving over the nearby hills. Between her legs, she cradled a bowl overflowing with acorns.

They had found the Oracle of Oak.

"We'll keep watch over the glen," Spraved said as she directed her fellow knights to form a circle around the tree, "but be quick. It's not safe to stay long in the open."

When the oracle saw Wily and his friends approaching, she stuck her hand deep into the bowl and pulled out a handful of the acorns. She shook them in her hand and then threw them down onto the wooden nest of roots before her. She leaned forward and, with childlike glee, examined each. She let out a loud hearty laugh of delight, as if she had just opened a gift she'd been hoping to receive.

"I see you found the trapsmith of Carrion Tomb," the Oracle of Oak said, her voice crackling like the knuckles of a bone soldier waking up from a long slumber in the crypts.

"Your acorns left out some very important details the last time we came to you," Odette said as she dismounted her horse. "Like the fact that Wily was also the son of the Infernal King."

"The acorns tell me all," the Oracle of Oak said. "But I am more selective with what I share."

"Let's cut to the chase," Valor said impatiently. "We need to find a tunnel that leads to the Below."

"Not so fast, young lady," the oracle said. "You need to pay me first."

Pryvyd reached into his pouch and pulled out one of the large sapphires Lumina had given them. He tossed it into the bowl of acorns.

The Oracle of Oak smiled, snatched an acorn off the ground, and bit down on it with her hard gray-blue teeth. The outer layer cracked open and she looked inside the broken nut. After a moment, she stuck her long fingernail into the dried pith and pulled out a small, slithering grub.

"What does it mean?" Pryvyd asked.

"It means nothing," the Oracle of Oak said. "They are just a good snack." She popped the squirming insect into her mouth. Her face puckered and her eyes watered. "Very sour," she said. "Like a berry before it's ripe."

The Oracle of Oak let out a laugh that was both full of joy and slightly unsettling. She swept her hand around the bowl of acorns, stirring them as if cooling a bowl of soup. She stared at the patterns that were forming. "There is a tunnel entrance to the Below at the western edge of the Black Lake," she said. "But you will not be able to pass through that one."

"Are there other tunnel entrances?" Odette asked.

Instead of answering, the oracle looked expectantly at Pryvyd until the knight tossed another sapphire into the bowl.

"Yes," the oracle responded. "There are four tunnel entrances to the Below. The Black Lake Tunnel. The Frenig Volcano Tunnel. The Frozen Desert Tunnel. And the Catacombs of Blood Tunnel. But stone golems stand guard at every one of them. Stalag already knows what you are planning."

"He does?" Wily asked. "How?"

"Because I told him," the Oracle of Oak replied as if it were the most obvious thing in the world.

"What?" Pryvyd asked alarmed. "Why would you do that?"

"You're a traitor to the whole land," Odette exclaimed.

"He paid my price," the oracle said. "He asked about tunnels to the Below. Just like you asked about tunnels to the Below. I told you both the truth. I answer the questions that are being asked."

Something in the way the Oracle of Oak phrased that last statement made Wily think of the Skull of Many Riddles. There was a clue hidden in what she had said. Wily moved to Pryvyd's side and grabbed a sapphire from the bag. He tossed it to the oracle.

"Is there any way of reaching the Below," Wily asked, "other than through a tunnel entrance?"

The oracle smiled. "Yes," she said. "There is a hole at the center of Frenig Volcano that will take you to the Below. Or at least part of the way there. There are no stone golems at the top of the volcano. Only at the bottom."

"Are you talking about the Lava Crown?" Odette asked. "There is no path to the center of the crown and no steps down it. Only the ash gulls fly in and out."

"That is the hole to the Below," the oracle said.

"Maybe we could fly in," Roveeka suggested. "Build a mechanical birk just like we did to get into the Infernal Fortress a few months ago."

"I've seen the Lava Crown," Odette said. "It's not wide enough for a mechanical bird to fly through. And besides, that mechanical bird was barely strong enough to lift Wily, let alone all of us."

"Could you quell a flying beast and get it to carry us down?" Roveeka asked Valor.

"Convince a giant eagle to fly into a ring of lava?"

Valor scoffed. "Animals have a strong sense of self-preservation. That will never happen."

"We need a bridge," Pryvyd said.

"It would be impossible to build," Wily countered. "We would need support beams. And those would just melt into the lava."

"Not if the bridge floated," Pryvyd said.

"How would that happen?" Odette asked.

"Halo wax," Pryvyd said. "A lot of it."

"I've never heard of it," Wily said.

"Because it is a sworn secret of the Knights of the Golden Sun," Pryvyd replied. "It lightens the load. A thimble of the wax smeared on our armor makes it light as a feather. It's how we never tire of wearing our armor or shields."

"I thought you were just really strong," Roveeka said.

"I'm strong too," Pryvyd said. "If you put enough halo wax on an object, it will float. Not high off the ground, maybe a few inches. But we don't need our bridge to float very high. Just enough to keep it out of the lava." Pryvyd called out to Spraved. "Was the wax vault breached at Halberd Keep?"

"Not when we left," she replied.

Suddenly, the roots of the blue oak began to shift, circling around the Oracle's waist and legs, forming what appeared to be the bottom half of an eggshell.

"Danger is coming," the Oracle pronounced. "When

the three horns arrive, there is but one thing to do. Sink into the mud."

The roots of the tree continued to loop around the oracle until it appeared as if she were sitting inside a large nutshell. Then the muddy ground opened up beneath the tightly wound shell and swallowed it whole. And just like that, the Oracle of Oak was gone.

"Great advice," Odette said with a sigh. "When danger comes, we can all just bury ourselves in the mud. That will save the land."

Wily looked down at the acorns the Oracle had left lying on the ground. He saw that they formed a very clear pattern on the ground. A three-horned helmet. A helmet that looked just like the one his father wore when he was the Infernal King.

*Is it just a coincidence they look that way? I'm sure no one else would see the same thing.*

"Is that the helmet of the Infernal King?" Valor asked.

*Or perhaps they would.*

"I think so," Wily said.

"So your evil father is part of this plan too?" Valor asked.

Wily didn't know what to say. He was wondering the same thing.

"Keep low," Spraved called out to the others. "Something or someone is coming."

# 13

# THE ROAD TO WAX
# AND FIRE

Wily's heart beat wildly as he scanned the hills for the danger that the Oracle had warned them about. Pryvyd tore the spiked shield off his back, while Righteous pulled out its sword. Roveeka slid her trusty knives, Mum and Pops, from her waistband. Odette plucked a fistful of purple mushrooms off Moshul's leg and prepared to toss them. Spraved and her soldiers held their spears at the ready. They waited expectantly, poised for battle. Only Valor stood nearby, relaxed and leaning against Stalkeer.

"What are you doing?" Roveeka asked Valor. "Didn't you hear what the acorn lady said?"

"That danger is coming," Valor replied. "I heard that. Only she didn't say when it was coming."

"I'm guessing pretty quickly," Odette said. "Why else would she disappear into the ground?"

"Because she's nuts," Valor said.

"She's an oracle."

"That doesn't make her any less weird," Valor said. "It might make her more so, actually. Look at the chipmunk over there."

Wily spied a small tree rodent sitting on a root, nibbling a nut.

"They can sense danger coming," Valor said. "And he's happily munching on his dinner."

Just then, Spraved pointed to the east. A figure was moving toward them in the darkness.

"Over there," Spraved whispered to Pryvyd.

As it approached, Wily could see the figure had horns sticking out from its head. It was coming their way.

"How did my father get free of the prisonaut?" Wily asked.

"He didn't," Valor said, squinting into the darkness. "That's an elk looking for a stream to drink from. If that's the evil force we're up against, I think we'll all survive to see another dawn."

As the figure got closer still, Wily could see Valor was right. It was nothing but a silver elk out for a graze. Everyone put down their weapons.

"Shall we go get this wax?" Valor asked as she mounted Stalkeer. "Or do we need to wait around until the dangerous elk passes?"

As Spraved guided the group north on their overnight journey, Wily kept looking over his shoulder, waiting for his father, the Infernal King, to come charging out of the brush with his spiked sword and electric ax. Once, while they were passing a cluster of berry shrubs, a flock of wild geese took flight and gave Wily a scare that made him almost fall off his horse.

But his father did not appear.

As morning arrived, Wily could see what looked like a small cluster of buildings surrounded by a ten-foot-high wall that was cracked and crumbling. Towering over it in the near distance was the Frenig Volcano, its peak glowing orange with bubbling lava.

"She's still standing," Spraved said, looking down at the keep. "Fortune is on your side today."

The Knight of the Golden Sun gave a nudge to her horse and galloped off for it. By the time Wily and his companions reached the entrance to Halberd Keep, Spraved had already had her knights open the gates for the visitors.

The plain gray outer walls of the outpost looked far different from within. The inner side of the walls held murals depicting various scenes from Panthasos's history—but the murals were in constant motion! There was a painting of Cloudscrape Peak, in which the wind blew puffy white clouds across the sky. Wily recognized another picture as the Floating City during a midday shifting. The Floating City was composed of hundreds of interconnected rafts that changed positions like a sliding tile puzzle. He stared at the mural as the city blocks moved across the lake in an elaborate dance of raft and pulley. If Wily had not known better, he would have thought he was staring at the city itself through a magical window. Some walls showed locations Wily didn't recognize, sandy islands with tall skinny trees that swayed in the ocean wind and snowy plains that seemed to stretch into infinity.

"These are to remind the knights what they're fighting for," Pryvyd said. "No matter how far they are from home, they can look at these walls and feel a bit closer."

As the group continued toward the center of the outpost, they passed a building with a painted wall that was stirring with colors but had yet to form a picture.

"What's this one supposed to show?" Roveeka asked.

"You see what you want to see in that one," Spraved answered. "Everyone finds something different in it."

Curious, Wily decided to inspect the mural more closely. He stared into the mix of colors. It was nothing but swirls of paint and dots of darkness. But as he kept staring, forms began to emerge out of the shapelessness. Little by little, a painting of a deep dungeon cave appeared before him. Sitting on a throne of bones was Stalag. He was surrounded by an army of stone golems so tall that they had to bend down to avoid scraping the tops of their heads against the ceiling. Sceely and Agorop were there too, along with a dozen other cavern mages standing in a circle, Girthbellow included.

Stalag had a large map laid out on the table. Wily

recognized the structure in the middle of it: the royal palace. He watched as one of cavern mages slid a black onyx figure across the map. He could see the figure was wearing a helmet with three horns.

"Is this showing what is happening now?" Wily asked Spraved.

"Sometimes it shows now. Sometimes it shows later."

Except for Odette, the others moved on to a large fortified structure at the center of the outpost.

"Why?" Odette asked. "What do you see, Wily?"

"Stalag plotting the fall of the royal palace," Wily said. "I think he may be working with my father." Suddenly, he felt all the pressures of the princehood come crashing down on his shoulders all over again. The scene melted in front of his eyes until it was once more only a swirl of spinning colors.

"We can hope that the mural just showed what will never be," Odette said. "I bet that's possible too."

Wily gave her a sad nod, not truly believing it. Then the two hurried to catch up with the others.

Spraved was using a key to open a padlock on a heavy wooden door there. She swung it open and beckoned them to enter.

Inside, Wily quickly discovered this was the armory. The walls were lined with hooks and brackets holding every kind of weapon, shield, and suit of armor imaginable. There were curved swords, double-sided battle axes, and pole arms as long as a giant's arm. Behind Wily hung shields of all sizes, some spiked and others smooth, each decorated with the golden insignia of the Knights of the Golden Sun.

Spraved led them past the armory and into a room where eight giant candles glowed brightly. As the wax melted from the wicks, instead of dripping down the side of the candles, it floated upward. The entire stone ceiling was coated in a thick layer of white wax that made it appear as if there were a cloud floating a few feet over Moshul's head.

"This should be enough," Pryvyd said. "Now we need a very large tarp and some tools to scrape this off."

Spraved brought in a half dozen spears and a huge tarp normally used to keep the rain from falling into the open horse stables. Everyone grabbed a long stick and began removing chunks of wax and tucking them into the doubled-over tarp. A few times Wily fumbled with a clump of wax and it went drifting back to the ceiling before he could grab it.

It didn't take long before the group had scraped half the ceiling clean. The tarp was now full of halo wax and hovering in front of them.

"This should be enough," Pryvyd said, tying the tarp into a large bundle, "to make our bridge to the center of the lava crown."

The group effortlessly pulled the light-as-air bundle of halo wax outside and attached it to the saddles of Odette's and Pryvyd's horses. The Knights of the Golden

Sun loaded Moshul's shoulders with dozens of thick coils of rope.

*BOOM!* Chunks of stone wall exploded all around them. A rock the size of an ale barrel nearly struck the horses carrying the halo wax. Wily looked to see a trio of stone golems attacking the southern wall of the keep.

Knights of the Golden Sun were grabbing their weapons and sprinting for the falling wall.

"You must leave," Spraved said. "We'll keep the golems occupied while you get away."

She approached Righteous, who was hovering near Pryvyd's shoulder.

"Keep your body out of trouble," she said.

Righteous gave her a thumbs-up.

"People change," Pryvyd said to Spraved. "Sometimes it just takes time. Or meeting the right friends."

The pounding of stone fists bashing against the walls was nearly deafening.

"Thank you for your help," Wily told Spraved. "Once we're gone, go to the royal palace. My mother will need your help. There are more golems than she and the royal guards can stop alone."

"We'll do our part," Spraved said. "You have nothing to worry about."

Wily could see the stern determination in her eyes, but he knew it would take more than resolve to defeat Stalag's army. They needed a lair beast. And soon.

"On the north side of the keep, there's an exit by the stables," Spraved said as she pulled her sword. "Go now."

Wily and the others hurried their mounts toward the stable as the sound of battle raged behind them. As they pushed through the exit, Wily turned one last time to see Spraved fighting single-handedly against a giant of stone ten times her size.

Valor was watching too. "Maybe not all wall-dwellers are bad," she said.

oOo

EVEN FROM A mile away, Wily could smell the pungent odor of lava bubbling up from the belly of Frenig Volcano. He'd grown accustomed to lava's distinctly smoky and rather unpleasant smell back when it had permeated every tunnel of Carrion Tomb. Even when there were other, stronger scents about, the odor lingered. There were very few things about his life in the tomb that he looked back upon fondly, and this smell was certainly not one of them.

As the companions moved closer to the base of Frenig Volcano, Wily could see two giant stone golems pacing back and forth near a large tunnel.

"That's the entrance we're not going to be getting through," Odette said. "The Lava Crown is at the top of Frenig."

She pointed to the upper ridge of the volcano, where smoke wafted into the sky.

"If we take Death's Tail," Pryvyd said, pointing to a trail of black rocks that wound itself off to the west before looping back toward the summit of the volcano, "we should be able to avoid being spotted by the golems."

"Death's Tail doesn't sound like a road anyone should be taking," Valor said with a roll of her eyes.

As they followed the trail closer to the volcano, Wily's nostrils began to tickle from all the floating ash. They moved slowly up the winding path toward the edge of the large black crater.

About halfway up the mountain, Roveeka began to squeal with delight. "Oooh! Yum!"

She was pointing toward a cluster of shambling gray beetles. As they squirmed across the cracked earth, they left a path of black smoke in their wake.

"What are those things?" Odette asked Wily.

"Sootslingers," Wily said. "Beetles that digest magma. They used to be all over the lava pits back in Carrion Tomb. Never had a problem getting rid of them though. The hobgoblets took care of that."

"They are a delicacy," Roveeka said, licking her lips. "You don't even need to cook them."

"They taste like the burnt bits of bread that fall into the fire," Wily said. "Never had a taste for them myself."

"How did you ever think you were a hobgoblet?" Odette asked.

"I admit that in retrospect I should have seen the clues."

Everyone shared a chuckle except for Valor, who remained stone-faced.

Wily pulled his horse up alongside her. "You don't have to be angry at me all the time," he said. "When are you going to give me a chance?"

"Are you kidding? This is me giving you a chance. Trust me when I say that I want to say terrible things. And yell and scream. But I'm not."

"I didn't do anything to you."

"You took my auntie away. She was the closest thing I had to a mother."

"That wasn't my fault."

"But that's how it feels. And it hurts. Just give me some space so I don't say the things that keep bubbling up inside me."

Valor gave Stalkeer a nudge ahead, leaving Wily to ride along Death's Tail lost in thought.

As they moved up the side of the volcano, he heard a voice call out. "There's not much of anything past here."

Wily looked around and near a pile of dried magma beheld the strangest of sights: a rat the size of Wily was standing on two legs like a person. It was filthy and held a large bucket in one of its claws. As Wily stepped closer, it hid the bucket behind its back.

"It's a skrover," Pryvyd whispered to Wily. "They're scavengers and liars and thieves. And not in a charming way."

"Nothing apart from lava rocks," the skrover continued, as his beady red eyes shifted about. "If it's sootslingers you're searching for, you'd have better luck trying the next volcano over. I caught all the ones up here weeks ago."

"What about that one?" Roveeka said, pointing to a large beetle shuffling through the dried lava. A trail of black smoke wafted from its body as if a fire were continuously being extinguished on its back.

"That's the last one," the skrover said, quickly scooping it up in his hairy claw. "All the rest are gone."

He bit down on the beetle, causing a puff of black smoke to drift from his nostrils. Wily pointed to another sootslinger pushing its way out of the dried lava. The skrover grabbed and devoured that one too.

"You can rest easy," Wily said. "We're not looking for sootslingers. They're all yours."

The skrover didn't look like he believed Wily.

"Really," Roveeka chimed in. "We're not. Despite how delicious they smell."

The skrover relaxed and allowed his bucket heavy with beetles to move to his side. "In that case, go right ahead," the skrover asked. "But what other reason do you have for going this way?"

"Just passing through," Pryvyd said.

"Actually," Roveeka added, "we've come here to enter the Below."

Pryvyd quickly cut Roveeka off. "The truth is we're

just passing through," he repeated, staring firmly at the hobgoblet. "To the plains beyond Frenig."

The skrover grabbed a sootslinger from his bucket and chomped down on its head. "Enjoy your trip to the plains," he said as he began hobbling down the hill. "Have a simply wonderful day. The best day you've ever had."

The skrover broke into a sprint, nearly tripping on rocks and dead tree roots.

"Well," Roveeka said. "He seemed very nice. I hope it is the best day ever."

# 14

## LAVA CROWN

It was a long climb to the top, and as they ascended, it got hotter and hotter. When they finally reached the summit of Frenig Volcano, everybody was drenched in sweat, and Wily could see that a massive, boiling lake of lava filled the crater almost to the rim. At the center of the pool was a large opening the lava poured into. Boulders dotted the edge of the lake.

"We need to get through there?" Roveeka said doubtfully.

"You heard the Oracle of Oak," Wily said. "That's the only unguarded way into the Below."

"We need to start coating these boulders in halo wax," Pryvyd said. "Then we'll line them up over the lava to make a path to the center."

"What will we do then?" Roveeka asked.

"Tie the rope to the last one and have a very long climb down," Pryvyd said.

They moved to a flat rock and opened the tarp full of halo wax. Together, all of them began slathering the airy wax all over the rock. Once it was slick white, to everyone's delight, the large stone hovered a hand's length above the lava. They pushed it to the lava lake and placed the hovering stone just a step from shore.

"Just ten more of those," Wily said, "and we will get to the center with no problem."

They hurried back and started coating a second boulder with the halo wax. After finishing, they moved it into place next to the first rock. As they started on the third rock, Wily heard a crash near his feet. He shielded his eyes as chunks of rock exploded all around him. When it was safe to look around again, he quickly spotted the two stone golems from the base of the volcano, who were now standing on the far side of the lava lake. Both of them were holding massive boulders in their hands and getting ready to hurl them at Wily and his companions. Standing next to them was the treacherous skrover.

"Where do you think you're going?" the taller of the two stone golems shouted, his voice echoing around the crater.

Roveeka suddenly looked very guilty. "I'm sorry," she said. "This is all my fault."

"It was a mistake," Valor said. "We all make them."

Roveeka smiled as Wily gave Valor a surprised look.

"*She* never did anything to me," Valor said.

The other stone golem tossed a second boulder at the companions, but Moshul was quick to react. He grabbed a nearby stone and lifted it in front of the flying rock to block it. The two boulders made contact and shattered into a thousand pebbles. Moshul was knocked off his feet and nearly smashed into Wily and Valor.

"Everybody onto the bridge," Pryvyd called out.

"But it's not finished," Odette said.

"There may be a way," Pryvyd said, grabbing the tarp full of halo wax.

Wily and the others left their horses and the mountain lion behind and stepped onto the first stone slab.

"Keep going," Pryvyd said, "onto the second block."

Odette led the way, then stopped short at the edge of the lava.

"Now what?" she yelled.

Pryvyd grabbed the first hovering stone block and moved it in front of them. They were going to get across the lava lake by moving the stone bridge pieces so there was always a block in front of them! Everyone quickly hurried forward.

Wily felt a surge of hope; they were actually going to make it! But he was surprised the stone golems hadn't continued bombarding them with more rocks. Then he looked up and understood: the two stone golems had lifted a giant chunk of rock up over their shoulders together. Wily watched them heave it into the air. The rock only flew a short distance, not nearly far enough to strike Wily and his friends, and plummeted into the lava lake. Wily almost laughed at their failed attempt.

It only took a second for him to realize the stone golems were in fact much smarter than he realized. They had never intended for the boulder to hit them. It didn't need to, because something else would: where the boulder had struck the surface of the lava lake, a gigantic wave of boiling lava had formed, and it was rolling right toward them.

The wave of lava moved at tremendous speed. Wily realized what was about to happen. The wave was going to come crashing over them and burn them alive.

"On the count of three," Wily shouted, "jump up."

"Why?!?" Odette said.

"One. Two. Three."

All of the companions jumped at the same time. When they came down together, their combined weight caused the hovering rock they were on to hit the lava with a splash, melting the wax right off the bottom.

"How was that a good idea?" Odette screamed. "The rock won't hover over the lava anymore."

"That's true," Wily said, "but now it can ride the wave."

The wave of lava kept rolling toward Wily and the

others. As it rose up behind them, the stone they were precariously balanced on tilted downward and was sent gliding across the lake's surface. The wave was licking the back of the stone, preparing to crash over them. But the floating bridge piece rushed ahead and just avoided being swallowed. As the wave crashed behind them, their stone ride was sent racing even faster across the lava—straight toward the hole in the middle of the lake.

There would be no gentle climb down a rope ladder. The hovering rock shot into the ring of lava, and they began to fall into the dark pit at its center. As they fell, Wily clutched the edge of the rock and looked over. The glowing circular waterfall of lava seemed to stretch down into infinity. The sight was positively dizzying. Wily wondered if this was what the bottomless pit of Carrion Tomb would have looked like if it had been lit up.

"We're going to die!" Valor shouted.

She was right. If they hit whatever was below them going at this speed, they would all be flattened—and unlike Moshul, they wouldn't be able to walk it off with a newly shaped back.

They needed some way to slow their fall. Unlike with their shield sled ride, there was nothing here for Righteous to attach a rope to. Wily's mind was spinning like a loose gear about to snap off. Then he spied the tarp of halo wax.

Wily lunged for Pryvyd and grabbed the tarp.

"Moshul, spread this overhead," Wily called out. "And everyone get on his shoulders."

Odette, Valor, Roveeka, Pryvyd, and Wily all jumped aboard Moshul as he extended his arms and opened the tarp still half-filled with halo wax.

The air was swept up into the cloth, forming a huge dome above them. Their rapid descent was instantly slowed. The rock went tumbling below as Moshul and his companions drifted down.

"That was brilliant, Wily," Roveeka said. "How'd you come up with that?"

"Paraspores," Wily answered. "The little fungus seeds would drift down from the cave ceilings using chutes shaped like domes."

As they continued to descend, the light of the sun faded above. Yet it wasn't dark: the flaming walls of lava dropping from the edge of the lake basked everything in a warm glow of orange. Wily felt his skin crackling with heat. He wondered if this was what a cookie felt like when it was baking in an oven.

As they sailed deeper and deeper into the volcano, Wily could see that the falling lava was caught in a basin that extended around the perimeter of the wall. It was like a giant fountain. The lava was swept into holes in the walls and likely sent back to the surface to bubble and fall once more. As they descended farther still, the hole darkened rapidly as there was no more lava surrounding them. Fortunately, the temperature began to decrease too.

A group of fireflies fluttered up from Moshul's thick moss. They lit up the small area beneath the parachute but not much beyond.

"How much deeper do you think this goes?" Roveeka asked.

"The say the Below is a land beneath even the deepest dungeon. I would imagine that we have a very great distance to travel yet," Odette said.

Wily spotted a few strange creatures peeking their heads out from holes in the stone walls. While he couldn't see them clearly, he guessed they were some kind of spider, judging by the fact that they were speaking in Arachnid.

"They look delicious," Wily heard one click. "Especially the large one in the golden shell."

"I would happily take the small pale ones," another spider voice mumbled. "Maybe not as much meat but the bones will be just as crunchy."

"We're not here to be eaten," Wily called out in Arachnid. "Find a different meal."

"Your Arachnid is very good," Valor said. "But trying to talk reason with spiders is wasted energy. They only appreciate a commanding voice."

"It's always worked for me," Wily answered. "Maybe

surface spiders like to be pushed around. But dungeon spiders appreciate being spoken to kindly."

"Get back to your webs, eight legs," Valor intoned. "Or I'll find a death mantis who would think you were the tasty meal."

Valor's booming voice was enough to give Wily chills down his back, and it seemed to work quite well. He could hear the spiders skitter away. Wily looked at Valor with reluctant admiration. She noticed, and they started to share a smile when—they hit the bottom of the cavern with a mighty thud.

"Is this the Below?" Odette asked.

"I don't think so," Roveeka said. "I don't see an upside-down star. But we certainly are deep."

Everyone climbed off Moshul's back and onto the floor of the pit. Roveeka moved swiftly into the darkness, leaving the others behind.

"Roveeka, where are you going?" Wily called out.

"Over here."

Wily followed the sound of her voice. The others followed behind him. Moshul's fireflies lit the path ahead until they found Roveeka standing by an arched doorway. Like all hobgoblets, she had a natural talent to see in the dark.

"This looks like the only way out of here," Roveeka said, pointing into a pitch-black tunnel.

"Do you think it is safe?" Wily asked.

"I don't think anything is safe down here," Pryvyd answered.

Moshul put his ear to the ground, but only for a moment.

"Do you hear something?" Odette asked.

Moshul began to sign to the others.

"He says he hears footsteps," Pryvyd said. "Hundreds of them. And they're moving this way."

# THE GRAND SLOUCH

Moving just a short distance down the tunnel, Wily could soon hear not only the footsteps Moshul had warned about but also the creak of wagon wheels. And through an opening ahead, he could see the light of flickering torches.

"Thash it," a familiar male voice called out. "Keep it moving. One, two, four, three. One, two, four, three."

"It's one, two, three, five, you idiot," a familiar female voice shouted.

Wily and Roveeka looked at each other.

"Agorop," Wily said.

"And Sceely," Roveeka answered.

There was no mistaking the voices of Carrion Tomb's oglodytes and their inability to count properly.

Wily walked carefully to the opening. He found himself looking down a wide passage holding a strange parade of villainy. Two lines of a hundred bone soldiers were dragging an enormous wagon, big enough to carry a full-size lobster dragon—although it was currently empty. A dozen boarcus walked alongside the soldiers, carrying torches to light the way. At the front of the line was a female cavern mage with a glowing walking stick that spewed green smoke. Sceely and Agorop were patrolling the lines of soldiers, each carrying a bullhorn through which they barked their orders.

The female cavern mage came to a stop at the far end of the passage, where two tunnels split off into the darkness. She reached into her cloak and pulled out an object that Wily couldn't quite make out from the distance. She mumbled something to herself, and suddenly Wily heard a loud and familiar whistle. She was using the enchanted compass! She pointed to the smaller of the two tunnels.

"Ish goin to be a par-tic-al-aly tight shqueeze," Agorop yelled into the bullhorn.

Agorop was correct: the mouth of the tunnel seemed barely wider than the wagon itself.

The cavern mage lifted her frail hands and pointed at the mouth of the tunnel. Suddenly, a pair of giant spectral hands formed. They grabbed the rock walls and pulled them wider as easily as if the walls were made of clay, adding several feet on either side.

"Never mind," Sceely shouted. "It won't be tight at all."

The bone soldiers slowly and steadily pulled the wagon into the expanded tunnel.

"They must be looking for neccanite," Roveeka said.

"And a whole lot of it, judging by the size of the wagon," Valor said.

"Stalag could make a lot of golems with that much," Roveeka said.

"We have to stop them," Odette said.

Righteous clearly thought so too. It pulled the sword from Pryvyd's sheath and swung it, ready for battle.

"Even if we could keep them from finding the neccanite," Valor said, "that won't stop the army of stone golems Stalag has already built. If we don't find Palojax and quell it, every animal in Panthasos will be in danger."

Righteous lowered its sword in disappointment.

"But if they build unbreakable golems, even the lair beast may not be able to help," Odette countered. "I think we should steal back the compass and end their hunt."

Righteous lifted the sword in the air once more with unbridled energy.

"I disagree," Valor said. "We can't be distracted. We should stay focused on the task at hand."

"I agree with Valor." Wily was surprised to hear himself uttering these words. Valor seemed surprised too.

Righteous turned back and forth between the companions, waiting to see what the others were going to say.

"I think Wily and Valor are right," Pryvyd said. "Let's find the Below and the lair beast."

Disappointed, Righteous slid its sword back into Pryvyd's sheath.

"Don't worry," Pryvyd said to Righteous, giving its floating shoulder a pat. "You'll get a chance to swing that sword again soon enough."

"And suddenly," Odette said to Wily as she looked over at Valor, "you two are agreeing with each other?"

"This time she's right," Wily said. "Maybe next time you will be."

Odette crossed her arms, clearly not pleased about being overruled.

Once the last boarcus had followed the wagon into the widened tunnel, Wily and his friends descended from their elevated perch and proceeded down the passage and into the tunnel that the cavern mage hadn't chosen. It began to slope down steeply, which seemed like a good sign. The only way they had to find the Below was to keep going deeper until they reached it.

As they walked, Wily's mind kept flashing back to the pattern of the acorns the oracle had left behind: the three-horned helmet of the Infernal King. *How is my father involved in all of this? Is it possible that he's been secretly organizing all this from his locked room in the prisonaut? Has he gotten out of the prisonaut using the stolen screwdriver?*

The tunnel eventually led them into a large dark chamber that was so big Moshul's fireflies weren't able to illuminate its other side. As they moved about the chamber, an explosion of red flames ignited from an urn in the center of the room.

Wily froze in place. Before them, a mold-ogre as tall as a stone golem stood against the wall. In the roar of the flames, Wily could see black slime dangling from its chin and limp fingertips. Clumps of fur sprouted from the eight toes that stretched out from each of its large feet. Its eyes shifted stiffly to face them.

Odette got into her fighting stance. Roveeka pulled out her knives. Valor snapped a pair of wooden arm claws onto the back of her hands. Righteous yanked its sword from Pryvyd's sheath.

Pryvyd looked to the floating arm by his side. "I told you, you wouldn't have to wait long," he said as he readied his shield.

A low, rumbling voice came from the mold-ogre's large closed lips. It spoke Gruntspeak, a language in which Wily was fluent. "You're lucky I've just eaten," the mold-ogre said. "Or you'd already be in my belly."

"We just want to walk peacefully through your cavern," Pryvyd said.

"Take another step toward me," the mold-ogre said, "and I will lick your bones clean." It slowly lifted a menacing eyebrow.

"We can offer treasure for safe passage," Odette said.

"No!" the mold-ogre shouted. "I want you to go back the way you came. I don't wish to be disturbed."

"Even great knights know when it's best not to fight," Pryvyd said.

Righteous turned to Pryvyd, clearly not pleased with his declaration.

"That's right," the mold-ogre said. "Go back the way you came."

Wily remembered the tentacled idol that stood in the first chamber of Carrion Tomb. It warned invaders to turn back, just like this mold-ogre was warning them. Wily stared through the darkness at the mold-ogre's slowly shifting eyes. He thought for a moment. Then he walked straight up to the mold-ogre and kicked one of its hairy big toes.

*CLONK.*

The toe wasn't a toe at all. It was hollow.

"This is not a real mold-ogre," Wily said. "It's made with wood and plaster."

"That's not true!" the mold-ogre bellowed. "I just haven't eaten in a while."

Wily looked up to the raised hand of the mold-ogre.

From this close, he could see the arm was being lifted by thick twine.

"And I suppose the ropes attached to your arms are on account of your lack of strength?" Wily asked. "I should compliment you on your sophistication," he continued. "A lot of craftsmanship went into it."

"You don't know what you're talking about," the mold-ogre muttered through his closed mouth. "If you don't leave, I will stomp you."

"What sort of mechanics did you use to make the eyes shift?" Wily asked. "Interlocking gears or levers?"

"Levers, of course," the mold-ogre uttered, then caught himself. "Oh, twiddle dump. Look what you made me say."

"We just want to pass through," Roveeka said. "We won't bother you."

"Where are you from?" the mold-ogre asked, suddenly very curious. "The Above?"

"Yes," Wily said. "We're just—"

"Not you," the voice cut Wily off. "I was asking the hairless girl. Are you from the Above too?"

"That's right," Roveeka replied. "At least, I'm recently from the Above."

"How'd you get in here?" the voice asked eagerly. "Did you come in through the tunnel at the base of the volcano?"

"We came down through the lava lake."

"HOOOO!" the mold-ogre called out.

Suddenly, Wily and the others heard a tremendous amount of rumbling and rustling. Then there was pronounced click. A secret door swung open from one of the mold-ogre's feet. A small, slouched figure, a little shorter than Roveeka and covered from head to toe in armor, emerged, holding a two-pronged spear in its hand. It moved steadily for Roveeka, who gripped Mum and Pops tightly in her fingers.

The armored figure peered out from its visor. "And you are a hobgoblet?"

Roveeka looked nervous. "Yes."

The armored figure removed his helmet to reveal that he too was a hobgoblet, slouched and bumpy, just like Roveeka. He lunged forward and dropped to one knee. Roveeka was startled and pointed both Mum and Pops at his face.

"Urgo, at your service," the armored hobgoblet said. He gently reached out, took the back of one of Roveeka's hands, and kissed it.

"This is weird," Roveeka said as she looked down at the armored hobgoblet.

"I'm going to have to agree with you," Odette said.

Urgo got to his feet and turned back to the mechanical mold-ogre. He cupped his hands around his mouth. "The Grand Slouch has arrived!"

Wily heard a burst of murmuring and excitement. Suddenly, rope ladders dropped out of the statue's nose. Secret doors on every toenail swung open. The jaw of the statue clicked open as well, and a collapsible wooden slide dropped out of the mold-ogre's lips and extended all the way down to the ground.

From the hidden compartments, dozens of hobgoblets came climbing, running, and sliding out. They were all cheering and repeating the same words over and over. "Grand Slouch. Grand Slouch. Grand Slouch."

"Why is everyone cheering as if they've just found the most valuable treasure in the world?" Roveeka asked.

"Because we have!" Urgo yelled. "You."

# 16

# UNDERTOWN

The hobgoblets, each with varying wart sizes and tooth lengths, gathered around the companions, waiting for a chance to get close to a very confused Roveeka and kiss her hand, like Urgo had.

"What is the Grand Slouch?" Pryvyd asked.

"She is! She is!" all the hobgoblets shouted in unison.

"We have been waiting for you," an older female hobgoblet called out from the crowd.

"We will return to the Above at last," another said.

"I'm sorry," Odette interjected, "but we really don't understand."

"You haven't heard the legend of the Grand Slouch?" Urgo asked incredulously.

Wily and the others shook their heads.

Urgo turned to Roveeka. "Surely, you know your own destiny."

Roveeka shrugged her sloped shoulders. "I'm just as confused as my friends."

The hobgoblets all looked at one another with shock.

"For two hundred and eighty-eight years, tales have foretold your arrival. Since the Flip of Decision when hobgoblets were sent down from the surface into the depths of the earth."

"Sent?" Valor asked. "I thought hobgoblets have always dwelled underground."

"Oh no," Urgo said. "We used to farm and till the land. Roam with the trees. Man and hobgoblet treated one another like brother and sister. But that all changed after an argument over a mushroom patch. The humans said it was on their land. The hobgoblets said it was on theirs. It was a fierce argument. But no one wanted a war, fighting, or bloodshed. That's when a wise young man made a suggestion.

"He said that both humans and hobgoblets should have their own countries. There was just one catch. To make room, one country would be underground and one would be on the surface. A golden coin would be flipped. On one side was a picture of a sun. On the other side was a picture of a cave. It would be called the Flip of Decision. The humans only requested to have the honor of being the ones to flip. The coin was tossed in the air and landed on the sun side. Hobgoblets keep their word, even if they don't like it very much. So down we went.

"And there were many good things down below. Valuable gems and the best-tasting grubs. Plus it was safe from the dragons that roamed above. But it was also dark and lonely. A dozen years later, a mischievous hobgoblet snuck to the surface on her own. She sought out a great prophet, the Oracle of Oak, with a single question. Would hobgoblets ever be allowed to return to the surface? The Oracle read a message from her magical—I can't remember what they're called—"

"Acorns," Roveeka said.

"Exactly," Urgo said with a smile. "The oracle said that one day a hobgoblet from the Above would come flying down through the ring of fire. That hobgoblet would turn back time and bring us to the surface again. Since that day, we've been waiting for what we named the Grand Slouch. Now you have arrived. And we will get our day in the sun once more."

Roveeka looked truly puzzled. "I'm no leader," she said. She pointed at Wily. "I'm just here to help my brother."

"She calls a human her brother!" Urgo said. "Just like in the olden days!"

"You will take us to the Above, Grand Slouch," the hobgoblets chanted. "You will turn back time."

"I suppose I could try," Roveeka said. "But I've never really altered reality before."

"Perhaps she could do that after we get to the Below," Odette interjected.

"If the Grand Slouch needs to go to the Below," Urgo said, "she can climb down the Million Rung Ladder. Then turn back time. Come with us!"

Urgo pushed through the crowd of bowing and curtsying hobgoblets toward one of the secret doors in the mechanical mold-ogre. "Move over," he said. "Grand Slouch coming through!"

As Roveeka passed through the throng, hobgoblets reached out to touch her.

"The big green guy and the tall human will need to take the long way around through the larger tunnels of the slime garden," Urgo said, "but the rest of you can fit through here."

Wily ducked his head and entered the narrow door in the mechanical mold-ogre's foot. The inside of the mold-ogre was a wonder to behold. Ropes and levers crisscrossed through beams and turning gears. These were the machines that made the arms, eyebrows, and eyes come to life. It was a feat of engineering that would have impressed even the most sophisticated locksage.

"Right this way," Urgo said as he led them toward a dark tunnel at the back of the giant contraption.

It became so dark that Wily could barely see his own hand. He had to walk with his arms outstretched, following the lumpy bumps in the wall.

"I can't see anything," Odette said. And a moment later, "Ew, I think I just touched a filthy fuzz spider."

"That's my hair," Wily said as he swatted her hand from his head.

"When was the last time you took a bath?" Odette asked.

"I've been a little preoccupied with saving all of Panthasos."

"I found time to rinse my hair at least."

After a few more bends in the darkness, Urgo, Wily, Valor, Odette, and Roveeka exited the tunnel into a huge cavern cast in an orange glow. As they came up and over the edge of the slight incline, Wily found himself beholding a magnificent sight.

Before him was a sprawling underground metropolis of hundreds of stone buildings. Some were built directly into the cave walls. Others were freestanding, leaning in all sorts of strange and uneven ways. Most were as curved and twisted as a hobgoblet's spine. It was almost as if the buildings were leaning on one another for support; Wily wondered if one toppled, would the others all come crashing to the ground? Even from this distance, he could see glowing rivers flowing through the city.

"Is that lava?" Odette asked.

"A long time ago," Urgo began, "we realized we couldn't keep the lava out. It would seep through the cracks in the walls if we tried to block it. So instead we decided to make it our friend. We welcomed the lava. We built alleys for it. There are some things that you cannot stop, so instead you must work around them. Now we cook our food with it. Warm our houses with it. And light our streets with it."

"It's beautiful," Roveeka said.

"We call this place 'Undertown,'" Urgo said. "Because it is a town that is under the ground."

"Yeah, I think we all figured that one out," Odette said.

"It's a very clever name if you ask me," Roveeka said.

As they approached the edge of the city, Moshul, Pryvyd, and Righteous reconnected with the group.

"Even the path we took was pretty tight quarters," Pryvyd said.

"It's our way to keep the 'bigs' from attacking our city," Urgo said. "If a huge monster can't fit through the tunnel, they aren't going to be able to attack the city. And to be quite honest, there are a lot of rather unpleasant creatures that live down here. It's easier to just keep them out."

As they entered Undertown, hobgoblet families peered out of their windows at the strange guests.

"This is the Grand Slouch," Urgo called out. "She's going to turn back time."

The group passed by a stand where a hobgoblet was selling soup. The soup ladler called out to Roveeka. "Soup for you? Black sludge soup. With or without cricket chips."

Roveeka happily took the sample and drank it in one gulp. "It's all gooey and gets stuck to the back of my throat." She turned to Wily. "Yum! I need to find a way to turn back time and bring the hobgoblets back to the surface just so I can get her a job in the palace kitchen."

"Yes," Urgo said, his voice full of joy. "We can all work in the palace kitchen!"

"We might be able to find some other jobs for you," Wily said, eyeing the unappetizing gruel in the black cauldrons.

"As you can guess," Urgo said, "there are not a lot of job opportunities down here in Undertown. We really have very limited choices. Every once and a while a cavern mage or a vile sorceress will make the trip down to hire some hobgoblets to work their dungeon. But that's only for the lucky few. What a happy life they lead!"

Wily looked at Urgo strangely. "How can you be sure that they're happy when they go to those dungeons?"

"It's obvious!" he said. "They never come back. They must be having such a wonderful time that they don't want to leave. Which is why we have been so eagerly awaiting the arrival of the Grand Slouch. So we will all have wonderful lives in the Above!"

Wily thought it might not be the best idea to tell Urgo the truth about what it was like working in a dungeon.

The group walked through the bustling streets of Undertown. Rumors of the hobgoblets' savior had spread like wildfire. Young hobgoblets came out of their houses to see the Grand Slouch and cheered as she passed.

"It's hard to have everyone looking at you with hope in their eyes," Wily said, worried Roveeka might be crumbling under the pressure of expectation.

"Hard?" Roveeka said. "I think it's wonderful."

"But you can't turn back time," Wily said. "Even cavern mages can't do that."

"I can figure something out," Roveeka answered.

"But what if you fail?" Wily asked. "They're all counting on you."

"My knife instructor always used to say, 'Sometimes you hit the target, other times you don't. But if you spend all day polishing your daggers, you won't hit anything at all.'"

Wily watched as Roveeka slouched proudly down the street with a crooked smile on her face. He was glad that little piece of advice made her feel better, because it certainly didn't make a lot of sense to him.

When they reached the edge of Undertown, Wily saw a deep hole with a heavy wooden ladder leading downward into an abyss. The ladder quickly disappeared into the total darkness below.

"This is the Million Rung Ladder," Urgo said. "It is named that for its . . ."

"Million rungs?" Odette asked.

"Yes. Exactly. How did you guess?"

"I'm starting to figure out how you guys come up with names for things here in Undertown."

Moshul walked up to the hole and gave the ladder a firm shake.

"I think it should be strong enough for you," Urgo said. "At one point, a hundred hobgoblets were climbing up and down the ladder at the same time. And you're not as heavy as a hundred hobgoblets, are you?"

Moshul touched his stomach self-consciously.

"Why don't you go down it anymore?" Wily asked.

"A hobgoblet wandered into the Below and was torn to pieces by Palojax, the lair beast," Urgo said. "But you guys have fun down there. And be sure to come back soon and turn back time."

Wily and Odette shared an uneasy look.

"Moshul, why don't you go first," Pryvyd suggested. "If you slip, I'd rather not be under you."

With a nod of agreement, Moshul took hold of the ladder. His fireflies spread from his body and drifted down into the pit. Wily followed right behind the moss golem. The rest came after him.

Wily had used ladders like this every day in Carrion Tomb and had learned a trick to make trips down them much swifter. He tucked his feet on either side of the ladder and let himself slide down. He knew how to hold the ladder so the palms of his hands were tucked into the bottoms of his sleeves to prevent splinters. After what still felt like an hours-long descent, Wily's feet finally touched solid ground. He stepped off the ladder and moved next to Moshul. They waited in the glow of his fireflies as, one after another, the others caught up with them.

Despite their long climb, it was hard to tell the difference between the dark tunnels above and these dark tunnels far below. They all looked the same to Wily. He and Valor took the lead, and the companions started down a sloping corridor.

As Valor walked alongside Wily, she looked around at the cold, damp tunnels. "I don't know how you did it," Valor said. "Being stuck underground without ever seeing the sun. It must have been horrible."

"There were a lot of good parts growing up underground," Wily said, feigning enthusiasm. He didn't want to give her the satisfaction of confirming how dreary it had been. "With no night and day, I never had a bedtime. And there are no mosquitoes in a dungeon. They can be really annoying and itchy."

"That's it?" Valor asked. "Those are all the good parts?"

"Plus, I got to spend a lot of time learning how to build things," Wily added. "If I hadn't been trapped underground, I might have been too busy doing other things."

"That's like saying 'It's great having a pocketful of rotten eggs because it keeps the skunks away,'" Valor said.

"I guess so," Wily said. Then he quietly asked, "What's a skunk?"

"It's like a black-and-white rat that can spray a horrible smell," Valor answered.

"Out of its mouth?" Wily asked.

Valor shook her head and pointed to her backside.

"Ewww," Wily said. "Animals from the Above are gross."

Valor let out a chuckle. Just as she did, Wily heard a distinct click. He knew that sound—he had heard it a million times in Carrion Tomb: Valor had just stepped on a pressure plate. He leaped forward to push her out of the way of whatever trap was about to strike. But before he could get to her, the floor dropped out from beneath the two of them.

# CHAMBER MUSIC

Wily and Valor dropped through the trapdoor and onto a stone slide slick with grease. Tangled in a mess of arms and legs, they slipped down into the darkness together. Far above, Wily could hear Odette and Pryvyd shouting, but their words were lost as Wily and Valor descended rapidly around and around the curving slide.

Valor's mouth was right next to Wily's ear as she screamed in terror. He realized this was the first time he had ever heard Valor sound scared. He didn't like it one bit, and it wasn't just because the scream hurt his ears.

"Press the balls of your feet against either edge of the slide," Wily shouted.

"Why?" she screamed back.

"Because we need to slow ourselves before we shoot

off the end of the slide into a pit of spikes or gurgling acid."

"I'm hoping there's a pile of goose feathers at the bottom," Valor said with fear in her voice.

"Unfortunately, it's never goose feathers," Wily yelled back. "Or pillows. Or a pool of sparkling fresh water."

Wily spread his legs and pushed his heels against the walls of the slide, but the grease was so thick it didn't seem to slow him at all. He tried using his hands and fingernails but couldn't get a grip. "Unless it's a pool of sparkling water with electric eels in it," he added. "That can happen sometimes."

Suddenly, the end of the slide arrived. Wily thought fast. He grabbed Valor's hand just as he left the edge and spun around midair to grab the lip of the slide. But he was too slow, his fingers narrowly missing, and both he and Valor went falling—

into a giant pile of pillows.

It took them a moment to realize what had happened. Wily looked at the pillows. Each was intricately woven with beautiful designs that matched the delicately painted patterns on the marble walls of the chamber. Wily patted the pillows with his hand. They weren't as soft as they appeared, but they were much softer than a pile of spikes.

"You were saying?" Valor said with a triumphant smile.

"Trust me," Wily said. "This never happens."

"It just did."

"Maybe these pillows are laced with sleeping powder," Wily said. "Otherwise it wouldn't be much of a trap."

"It's not a trap," a gentle voice said from the far side of the marble room. "It's a welcome slide."

"It's how we greet all our guests," an equally melodic voice explained from the other side of the pillows.

Wily looked up to see a pair of tall elves with pearl white hair and pale yellow skin. Both of them were sparkling as if they had been dusted in gold powder. The younger wore a light purple dress and the older one a heavy gown made of small ringlets of metal.

"Oh my," the elf in purple said. "You're not dirty hobgoblets or trolls. What an unexpected treat!"

"Yes," the one in the metal gown said. "A treat!"

"Actually, hobgoblets are quite lovely if you get to know them," Wily said.

"You're funny," the elf in purple said.

"Very funny," the other echoed.

"I am Gurta," the elf in purple said, "and this is my mother, Sytle."

"Hello," Sytle sang like it was the last note of a song.

"It is a pleasure meeting you both," Valor said politely. "If it's not too much of a bother, could you just guide us back to where your . . . welcome slide . . . opened suddenly and sent us tumbling downward?"

"Of course we will," Gurta said.

"We will guide you there right now," added Sytle.

"But first they should join us for a chamber piece," Gurta said to her mother.

"Yes," Sytle agreed. "A chamber piece. You'll love our musical gifts."

"Perhaps," Wily offered, "another day? We're a little pressed for time just now."

"We insist," Gurta said sternly as her eyes began to glow a sinister red.

"You must," Sytle added.

Gurta took a heavy breath and then her eyes went back to the innocuous white that they were before.

"Just follow us," Gurta said, her voice melodic once more.

The elfin mother and daughter walked in lockstep toward the door of the chamber. They gestured Wily and Valor to follow.

"We need to get away from this creepy duo," Valor said. "I have a really bad feeling about them."

"I don't see what choice we have," Wily said.

"We could knock them over the heads and make a run for it."

"We have no idea how to get out of here," Wily countered. "We can't go back the way we came. For now, I think we should follow them."

Valor clearly wasn't happy but wasn't able to come up with a better plan, so they followed the elves and found themselves in a well-lit cavern decorated with bubbling fountains and ornately carved statues. A twisting path led to a delightful cottage with stained-glass windows and a gently smoking chimney.

Valor and Wily spotted a pack of puppies playing at the side of the pool.

"Well, those are absolutely adorable," Valor said. She moved to the edge of the path and was about to step off when—

"Don't disturb them," Gurta said. "Stay on the path."

"Yes, stay on the path," echoed Sytle.

Valor gave a short bark to grab the puppies' attention, but they seemed too busy playing to notice her. After another unanswered bark, Valor shrugged and continued with Wily along the path toward the cottage.

"So is it just the two of you who live here?" Wily asked.

"Yes," Gurta said. "I live with the most wonderful person in all of Panthasos."

"Yes," Sytle added. "The most wonderful."

"You two are certainly a lot alike," Valor said.

"What a compliment," Gurta said.

"So flattering," added Sytle.

"Every daughter ends up just like her mother," Gurta said. "And every son becomes his father. It's a fate you can't escape."

"Yes," Sytle added. "Always the same."

Wily thought about his father and the terrible king that he had been. It was his greatest fear that he would end up like him. Was there really no escaping it?

As they got closer to the cottage, a pair of magical glass doors with glowing crystals swung open on their own. Wily could see that the cottage's interior was decorated with lovely furniture and artwork. Happy pictures of the mother and daughter lined the walls. After they entered the house, Gurta closed the door behind them. Wily heard the telltale click of a bolt slotting into place and knew they had just been locked in.

"We know you are in a rush," Gurta said. "But what kind of hostesses would we be if we didn't entertain you first?"

Wily and Valor reluctantly took their seats in large, ornate, overstuffed chairs as the two elves moved over to a large stringed harp and a pair of metal chimes.

"What song would you like to hear?" Gurta asked.

"I'm not really familiar with chamber music," Wily said.

"You're heading for the Below, correct?" Gurta said. "Then perhaps you would be interested in the piece known as 'The Great Below.'"

Gurta, with great excitement, began to pluck the notes of her harp. Her song was off-key and rather unpleasant. Wily could easily imagine he would do better than she without much practice. Sytle was using a small mallet to hit a row of the metal chimes, but was doing it so softly that the chimes didn't appear to be making any sound at all. Which, assuming she shared her daughter's lack of musical talent, was probably all for the better.

After a few minutes of the unpleasant melody, Gurta stopped plucking the harp. Wily and Valor began to clap, but Gurta looked at them sharply. "Why are you being so rude?" Gurta asked. "My mother is in the middle of her solo."

Wily looked over to see Sytle playing the chimes in a complicated pattern with a very intense face. But the music was so quiet Wily couldn't hear it at all.

After another minute of awkward silence, Gurta joined in again. The song reached an unpleasant crescendo, then stopped. Wily and Valor looked over to Sytle again.

"Why aren't you clapping?" Gurta asked.

"We weren't sure if it was done," Wily said.

"We stopped playing," Gurta said. "That's usually a pretty good sign that the song has ended."

Wily and Valor clapped politely.

"They didn't like it," Gurta said.

"They didn't like it," Sytle agreed sadly.

"No," Wily said a little too strongly. "We loved it."

Both daughter and mother shared a satisfied smile. They stood up in unison, took each other's hands, and curtsied, Gurta with her left hand and Sytle her right, as if they were perfect mirrors of each other.

"We do love the company," Gurta said.

"Yes," Sytle added. "The company is lovely."

Gurta let out a yawn. As she did, Wily caught a

glance of something odd out of the corner of his eye. One of the pillows on the chair he was sitting on suddenly changed into a gray, lumpy burlap sack. Gurta caught sight of the pillow and quickly shook her head as if to wake up again. Wily saw the sack was gone, back to the ornate pillow it had been before.

"We should all get some rest," Gurta said.

"Yes," Sytle added. "Some rest."

"I'm not actually tired," Valor said.

"I said 'rest'!'" Gurta screamed. Then, quickly, she resumed her pleasant tone. "Put these on, and in the morning I can—we can—set you on your way."

She handed blindfolds to Valor and Wily.

"I'm not wearing this," Valor said.

Gurta came right up into her face. "I need to sleep and that means you are going to sleep too."

Gurta let out another giant yawn. As she did the entire room flickered, and the beautiful ornate cottage suddenly transformed into a desolate, dreary house. Wily saw that he was sitting on a wooden bench covered with lumpy bags of burlap. The front doors were made of iron, not glowing crystals.

Wily scanned the room. The entire house had been transformed by an illusion. Most unsettling of all was that when the illusion had flickered out so had Sytle. Wily turned to the corner of the room. There, slumped against a wooden chair, was a skeleton that still had a metal ringed gown on it—the same dress that Sytle had been wearing. Or perhaps the same dress the illusion of Sytle had been wearing.

Gurta stomped toward them. "Why didn't you just put on the blindfold?" Gurta growled. "Why does no one ever put on the mask?"

Suddenly, Gurta's own appearance began to flicker. She was no longer a glowing beauty but instead a haggard and wild-haired old elf missing all her teeth. "You'll keep me company now," Gurta said. "Forever."

She reached out for Wily's wrist, but before she could grab it, Valor slapped her hand away.

"You're not keeping him, or me either," Valor said.

"I will not spend another day alone," Gurta said. "You will keep us company. Right, mother?"

Gurta looked to her mother's skeleton slumped in the chair and waited in vain for her to respond. Valor seized the opportunity to give the haggard elf a kick to the stomach, sending her tumbling backward.

Valor ran for the front door, pulling Wily behind her. Once they got closer, Wily could see that the iron doors had actually been shut with a heavy padlock. Valor began hitting it with the side of her fist, but no fist was going to break that lock open.

"Let me handle this," Wily said.

"What, you think you're stronger than me?" Valor asked.

"Definitely not," Wily responded. "You're way tougher than I'll ever be. But I'm pretty handy."

He pulled a pair of arrowtusk lock picks from his belt. He found the one with the finest point, stuck it into the lock hole, and twisted it until he heard a *click*. The lock snapped open. He thought back to how his father had used a screwdriver to escape from his shackles.

"Not bad," Valor said.

"Machines are a lot like beasts," Wily said. "They each have their own personality."

Valor gave the door a hard shove with her shoulder, forcing it open.

Wily looked out and saw not a beautiful garden and path but instead an elevated stone pathway with no sides that twisted its way through a dark, spooky cave. On either side of the elevated path, the ground was covered in cave urchins, black spiky crawlers with needlelike projectiles sticking out from their backs and heads. Wily knew they were not only sharp but poisonous too. A single touch was enough to stiffen muscles and make running, walking, and especially climbing impossible.

Wily and Valor ran out of the horrible haunted house and began winding their way along the twisting elevated pathway. Down below, the vicious urchins shuffled over each other, feeding on an unfortunate bat that had flown too low.

"This is the way we came," Valor said pointing to the left side of a forking elevated pathway.

"And it's a dead end," Wily said, "that leads only back to the slide."

"Good point." Valor turned to the right.

The elevated pathway may have been twisty but at least it was wide enough that if they stayed in the center, there was no chance they would accidentally fall off.

"You can't leave me!" Gurta shouted from the entrance to the house, holding a club made of urchin spikes.

"She won't be able to catch up with us," Valor said reassuringly as she looked over her shoulder. "Not if we keep up this pace."

Wily looked back to see Gurta transforming into a glowing red specter. A glowing sphere surrounded her and began to grow rapidly. It quickly overtook the house, transforming it into a frightening mausoleum. The glowing sphere continued to spread, changing everything in its path.

"It's just an illusion," Valor said. "It's not real. It can't hurt us."

Wily watched the bright shell of the illusion come rushing toward them. In a flash, the spell overtook them. The elevated pathway no longer looked like what it actually was—it appeared to be a regular, bland cave floor, flat and unimpressive. Which meant it was totally impossible to tell where the elevated pathway ended or began. It now blended in perfectly with everything else.

"Don't move," Wily said.

"I'm not going anywhere," Valor said. "You didn't happen to memorize the pathway to the exit, did you?"

"No such luck," Wily said.

Behind them, Gurta was running along the twisted elevated pathway that it seemed only she could see. Despite the seriousness of the situation, Wily couldn't help but think that Gurta looked ridiculous as she wove her way around what looked like a completely flat, wide surface.

He had to think fast. His trapsmith belt must have something he could use. He dove into the pouches and found screws and vials of goo, a hammer, and extra gears. Nothing that could help guide their way. Then he spotted Valor's feed pouch.

"I need birdseed," Wily said.

Valor held back a sarcastic remark and handed over the pouch.

Wily reached in, pulled out a handful of seed, and tossed it onto the ground before them. Some of the seeds appeared to stay on the surface while others disappeared.

"Only walk on the spots where you see the birdseed," Wily instructed Valor.

She nodded and followed Wily's lead. Every few steps, he threw another handful of seeds before him. Some landed on the elevated pathway, while the rest disappeared into the illusion.

"This is taking too long," Valor said.

Gurta was rapidly approaching with her urchin spike club.

Wily tried tossing birdseed as fast as he could. He gave Valor a handful to toss as well. They moved swiftly to the exit ahead.

"We're almost there," Wily said, looking to the stone arch that was coming closer and closer.

Valor looked back over her shoulder again and stopped in her tracks.

"She's gone," Valor said, clearly confused.

Valor was correct; Gurta was nowhere to be seen behind them. But when Wily turned around again to face the exit, Gurta was standing just a few feet in front of Valor, who screamed in surprise. Wily looked closer at Gurta and could see that her feet were hovering a few inches above the ground.

"Valor," Wily shouted, "that's not the real Gurta. It's just an illusion!"

The illusion of Gurta lunged at Valor. The shock sent her stumbling back. In a flash, Wily watched as she disappeared into the floor.

Wily ran to the spot where she'd fallen. Had she dropped into a pile of venomous cave urchins? He went to his knees. "Valor?" he said, trying hard not to panic.

"I'm right here," Valor said, her voice far closer than Wily had expected.

Wily saw the tips of her fingers rise above the illusion of the flat cave floor.

"I was able to catch the edge," Valor said. "But my hands are slipping."

Wily stuck his hands into the illusionary floor, reaching for Valor's hand.

"Can you see my hand?" Wily asked.

"Yes," Valor answered. "I can see everything under here. And it's not pretty. Keep your hand in one place."

Wily waited. Then suddenly he felt a hand grab his wrist tightly.

"I'm going to pull you up," Wily said. He heaved with all his might, pulling Valor out of the illusion and back up to solid ground.

"That was close," Valor said.

The illusion of Gurta held both of her hands up to signal them to stop.

"You cannot escape," the real Gurta screamed from somewhere behind them.

Wily grabbed Valor by the wrist, and together they ran straight through the illusionary elf. Wily kept tossing more birdseed on the floor until they reached the stone arch that appeared to signal the end of Gurta's realm.

The two kept running into the dark tunnel ahead. Wily pulled out a flint stone and candle to light their way. As he did, he noticed Valor staring at him.

"We just escaped," Valor said. "Why don't you look happy?"

"It was just something that Gurta said," Wily replied. "That a son becomes just like his father."

"Gurta is a crazy old elf. She doesn't know what she's talking about. You don't have to follow in your father's footprints. You could follow in your mother's. Or make your own path."

Wily listened carefully, Valor's words sinking in deeply.

"You are nothing like the Infernal King," Valor added.

Wily couldn't help but smile. Her words seemed to lift a heavy burden from his shoulders.

"And thanks for your help back there," Valor said.

"Of course," Wily said. Then he said something that surprised him. "It's what friends do for each other."

"You know, I really want to stay angry at you," Valor said with a grin. "But you're making it very hard."

## 18

## NEARLY BELOW

Wily wasn't sure how long they had been wandering through the maze of tunnels, but the candle was now not much more than a puddle of wax and a wick.

"This is new," Valor said, pointing to a patch of pale green vegetation dangling from the ceiling. "At least we know that we're not going in circles."

"I've actually never seen anything like this before," Wily said. "It's not cave moss or lichen or even a fern." Wily looked closer at the tuft until he was sure. "I think it's grass," Wily said.

"Growing on the ceiling?" Valor asked. "In a tunnel hundreds, if not thousands, of feet below the ground?" She stretched on her tippy-toes to get a proper look herself. "It doesn't make any sense," she added. "Grass needs sunlight to grow."

"Or an upside-down sun's light," Wily said.

He covered the top of the candle with his hand. In the dimness, he could see there was another source of light glowing softly from down the tunnel.

"The Below," Valor and Wily said in unison.

The two moved swiftly in the direction of the glow. Wily had never seen a light quite like this underground. It was warm and yellow, not so different from the rays of the sun shining through a distant, milky window. As they progressed, the grass on the roof of the cave tunnel got thicker and the light grew brighter.

Ahead, hanging from one of the green blades, was a white sphere about the size of a human head. Wily didn't need to get any closer to recognize it was an egg. But not a hard egg like a bird's or reptile's; this one was soft and gooey like the eggs of a giant spider. Wily looked around for more of the dangling eggs.

When he turned back to the first, it was gone.

"That can't be good," Wily said.

Out from the walls, ants the size of wolves began to emerge. They snapped their pincers as their antennae waved wildly in the air.

"What are they?" Valor asked as she backed away.

"I thought you would know," Wily said. "You're the quellmaster."

"And you're the one who's lived underground his whole life."

"Never seen them before," Wily admitted as he retreated.

"Congratulations to us both," Valor said. "We just discovered a new animal."

"I'm not feeling very excited by our find right now," Wily said as the large ants approached.

"I'll give you the honor of naming the species," Valor said as she slipped her wooden claws on.

"Wolf ants," Wily said.

"I think you can do better than that," Valor said.

Wily looked at the incoming swarm, snapping the air with their pincers. "Razor-beaked death ants?"

"That's accurate enough, I guess," Valor said.

Wily could hear more ants approaching from every direction. They were surrounded with nowhere to turn.

"What about 'ambush ants'?" he volunteered.

"Yep," Valor said, stepping between Wily and the nearest group of ants. "That's the name to go with."

"Can you quell them?" Wily asked.

"They're defending their young," Valor said. "Their instinct to protect their family is far stronger than any-thing I can do to calm them."

As if to prove she was right, the first group of ants skittered toward Wily, attempting to bite his legs and waist. Valor came to his defense, slicing the air with her wooden hand claws. Her right-hand blade sliced off the antennae of three of the ambush ants. With her other hand, she punched the head of a snapping ant. The claws made a loud cracking sound as they pierced the ant's hard outer shell. The giant insect collapsed to the ground.

"I must really like you," Valor said, "because normally I wouldn't hurt a fly."

"Maybe if the flies were as big as dogs and swarming around you," Wily said, "you'd change your mind about that."

Valor smacked another ambush ant away with her wrist claws. Just then, one of the ants bit down on Valor's ankle, breaking skin. Wily grabbed a hammer from his tool belt and smashed the ant attacking Valor on the side of the head. The ant crumpled as another took its place.

Valor was wincing from the pain of the bite and clutching her ankle. "I've got a new name for these damn bugs," Valor said, "but my uncle doesn't like me using that kind of language."

Wily looked down to see that Valor's ankle was swelling to the size of a grapefruit and turning as purple as a plum. Despite her worsening injury, she continued to swipe at incoming ants.

"I shouldn't have been so mean to you," Valor said.

"Apology accepted," Wily said.

"Hold your breath!" a voice screamed from behind Wily and Valor.

A purple mushroom exploded at Valor's feet. Wily covered his nose with his fingers. The ambush ants began to scramble away from the smoke—and from Odette and Moshul, who came charging down the underground corridor. Odette ran along the backs of the swarming ants toward Wily and Valor. Moshul squashed the ant reinforcements as they came streaming out of holes in the walls.

Odette reached Wily and Valor's side and snatched up the limp body of one of the dead ants. She used it to create a barrier between them and the other incoming ants. "What are you doing going into battle without us?" Odette asked, then coughed from the faint mushroom fumes still wafting through the air.

"How'd you find us?" Wily asked.

"Moshul had his ear to the ground," Odette replied. "We've been looking for you since you fell down the trapdoor."

Wily heard the sound of snapping above. He looked up to see an ambush ant preparing to drop down on him. Just then, Righteous came flying down the hall. The floating arm's sword pinned the ant to the wall. Its six legs squirmed helplessly.

Next came Pryvyd with his spiked shield, battering a path for himself and Roveeka. The hobgoblet was tossing Mum and Pops at ants as they popped out from holes all around the tunnel.

As Moshul came to a stop near Wily, Valor, and Odette, a line of tiny ants crawled out of the golem's belly button and down his leg to the ground. The small ants approached the big ants with waving antennae.

After a moment, the ambush ants retreated into the walls.

"Sometimes the littlest things," Pryvyd said, "can get you out of the biggest trouble."

The trail of tiny ants crawled back up Moshul and disappeared into his soft dirt body. Then Moshul turned to Wily and signed something with his big mossy hands.

Pryvyd translated. "Moshul was worried sick about you."

"We all were," Roveeka said.

"I wasn't really," Odette said. "I knew you'd be fine."

But Wily could tell by the way she gave him a giant squeeze that she had been very concerned as well.

Then she whispered in his ear. "To tell the truth, I was most worried about your being stuck with Valor," she said. "I thought you might kill each other."

Wily looked over at Valor. "Actually," he said, "that was probably the only good part about getting lost down here. She's actually amazing . . . once you get to know her."

Odette raised an eyebrow in surprise.

But Wily could see Valor wasn't doing so well. The swelling on her ankle was getting even larger.

"That doesn't look so good," Roveeka said, stating the obvious.

"It'll be fine," Valor said, attempting to walk. Her knee quickly buckled under the pain.

"Here," Wily said, pulling the healing water from the pool above Spider Rock out of his pouch. "Drink this. I don't need to grow a few more inches anyway."

Valor smiled and drank it down. "It'll still take a little while for the leg to heal," she said.

Odette turned to Moshul and signed to him, then turned back to Valor. "Moshul will carry you until it does." Odette turned to Roveeka next. "Looks like you're not the slowest member of the team anymore. You've got to carry yourself."

"No problem," Roveeka said. "I'm the Grand Slouch."

"As if one royal teammate wasn't bad enough," Odette said.

Righteous came flying up to the group and began pointing toward the soft yellow light in the distance.

"I think Righteous has found something," Pryvyd said.

Moshul picked up Valor and tucked her under his arm. Then the group hurried ahead toward the brightness. They reached a sloping path that curved like a spiral staircase downward. Wily could see that it was brighter below.

As they made their twisty descent, it grew even brighter and brighter. Soon it was as if the group was standing outside in the shade during a sunny day.

Wily came to the bottom out of the spiral ramp and found himself on a high rocky ledge looking out upon another extraordinary sight. He was in a massive cavern as wide as a thousand fields. The stone floor of the cavern was splintered like a clay vase dropped from a great height. Some of the cracks appeared slender enough to hop over, while others were so wide that no bridge would be long enough to stretch across the gap. Through the cracks, Wily could see a glowing yellow surface that was almost too bright to look at directly. It radiated heat and light upward, which helped to explain an even more bizarre sight.

The ceiling of the cavern was filled with tall pine trees hanging upside down. Their roots were buried in the ceiling above, while their branches of green leaves extended downward, soaking in the warm rays of the hidden sun. Flocks of pink-hued bats fluttered from tree to tree. Wily even thought he saw a few furry creatures hiding among the bigger branches.

"This is not quite what I was expecting," Odette said. "I thought we'd find a frightening place filled with terrible beasts slithering through mazes of sharp rocks."

Something about the Below felt incredibly calming to Wily. "I know this place," he said. "I used to dream about a trapless, treasureless dungeon where I could live peacefully. I think this is what I used to imagine."

"I remember you talking about a place like that," Roveeka said with a crooked smile.

"I guess it really existed after all," Wily said with a sigh.

"Before we get all cozy," Pryvyd said, "let's wait until we see what's crawling down on the surface."

"It's true," Valor said from the crook of Moshul's arm.

"We know Palojax must be down there somewhere. I don't think any of us should get too comfortable."

"Over there," Odette said, pointing to a set of natural stairs that led down to the surface of the Below.

The group began their descent. As Wily embarked on the long climb down, he expected to feel the heat start to increase. Instead, it felt just like a warm spring day. The only sweat dripping from his brow was caused by the couple hundred steps he was walking down. He wondered what magical force had created this underground sun.

When Wily touched down on the surface, he dropped to his knees and held his hand a few inches off the ground. To his surprise, it felt as cool as a rock in the shade. "It doesn't seem possible," Wily said. "Anything this bright should be as hot as a million ovens."

"The sun can be out on a winter's day," Valor said. "It's certainly not hot then."

"That's because the sun is so far away in the winter," Wily said.

"There's a lot we don't understand," Pryvyd said. "And we have to accept that we may never."

"Science can answer most of our questions," Wily countered.

"And magic answers the rest," Pryvyd replied.

Wily moved over to one of the cracks in the ground and tried to look directly into the upside-down sun. It was too bright to stare at for even a brief moment.

"Shall we find that lair beast?" Odette asked impatiently.

Wily nodded and pried himself away. The group began to move along the surface of the Below, circumventing the larger cracks in the ground. It was like navigating through a maze with no walls.

Then Odette let out an excited yelp. "Treasure!" she exclaimed, hustling over to a wide circle of gold nuggets piled ankle-high. "And it's just sitting here unguarded!" She grabbed a fistful of the gold.

"That's not treasure," Roveeka said. "Those are wishes." She pointed to the ceiling. A large hole stretched upward into the darkness. "This is the bottom of a bottomless pit," she said. "And these are hobgoblet wishes. Maybe one of these is mine. And maybe one is Wily's."

Odette looked at the gold in her hand. After a moment, she put it back in the circle. "You really know how to take the fun out of finding gold," she said to Roveeka.

"It's not real gold anyway," Roveeka added. "It's pyrite. Fool's gold."

"Nothing foolish about it," Wily said. "This gold makes dreams come true." He picked up a piece of pyrite and played with it.

Roveeka picked up a piece as well. "I wish I could turn back time," she said, "so that all the hobgoblets could live on the surface again."

"What are you wishing for?" Pryvyd asked Wily.

"That I'll make a great king one day," Wily said.

"Too late," Pryvyd said. "You already are."

"I wish we find Palojax soon," Odette said.

Just then, Valor pointed back to the ceiling. "Wish granted."

There, hanging upside-down from the ceiling, was a winged beast twice as black as the darkest block of nec-canite. It had leathery batwings wrapped around its body and three heads. Even from this distance, it seemed impossibly huge.

"Was that in your dreams of a trapless treasure-less dungeon too?" Odette said, swallowing hard.

Palojax unfurled its wings, revealing its tentacle-covered body. This creature was from no dream Wily had ever had before. Yet he was quite sure that, from this day on, it would be in his nightmares.

# 19

# THE LAIR BEAST

As Palojax flew closer, Wily's fear of the lair beast only grew. The three heads of the massive beast were now clearly visible—and how Wily wished they weren't! The left one resembled a fiery cobra with red and orange scales that flickered like a burning flame. The right head was a pale white bear's with blood-stained teeth. The center head, the frightclops, was the most horrifying of all. It resembled the face of a boarcus with tusks, floppy lips, and the nose of a pig. Yet, unlike any creature Wily had ever seen, it had a single eye buried in its forehead and a transparent skull that revealed the pulsing brain inside.

Moshul put Valor down on the ground and signed to Pryvyd.

"No," Pryvyd said as he signed back. "It's far too late to turn back now."

Moshul continued to sign.

"I'm scared too," Pryvyd replied. "And not just because he has tentacles."

Moshul shuddered at the word.

As if the three heads weren't terrifying enough, Wily saw, at the back of Palojax's body, a massive tail with a spiked fleshy ball at the end. As the creature flew, the mighty sphere moved back and forth like a pendulum. It looked as if the tail alone could knock an entire palace down to its cornerstones.

Roveeka pulled Mum and Pops from her waistband.

"I don't think those are going to do much," Odette said.

"I know," she replied. "It just makes me feel better to hold them."

Wily turned to Valor, who was standing tall despite her hugely swollen ankle. "Can you even walk on that?" he asked.

"I can walk, climb, and jump," Valor said. "It just hurts. A lot." She leaned her weight down on her ankle and winced. "An awful lot," she corrected herself. "But don't worry. I'll get on the back of that lair beast. I'm just going to need you guys to distract him."

"Okay," Wily said. He turned to Roveeka. "We may need Mum and Pops after all."

The hobgoblet held the blades up to her ears, then pretended to listen to them. "They are ready to fly," she said with a crooked smile.

"Hey, Wily," Odette called out. "You still holding on to that wish?"

Wily looked down at the cube of pyrite in his hands. He nodded.

"Because," Odette continued, "we might need it right now."

The lair beast dropped to the ground with an echoing boom.

"In fact, we might need the whole darn pile of them."

The three heads of Palojax each scanned the intruders, snarling angrily. *This is the moment of truth,* Wily thought. They would either find a way to succeed, or they would die, and Panthasos would have nobody to protect it from Stalag's army of stone golems. Wily Snare looked at each of his fine companions in turn, wishing he had spent more time with each of them. Odette stood next to him, clutching a pair of mushrooms that she'd plucked off Moshul's back. Righteous floated at the very front of the group, swinging its sword as if to say "Don't mess with us." Pryvyd stood behind Righteous, his spiked shield held aloft. Roveeka was on Wily's other side, putting on a very tough face. Since being named the Grand Slouch, a great confidence had radiated from within her. Moshul stood tall with spikes protruding from the vines stretched tightly around his chest, only flinching slightly at the lair beast's rows of squirming tentacles.

And Valor—where was Valor? She'd disappeared, which seemed impossible on this completely flat terrain. But she truly was nowhere to be found.

Then the frightclops, the center head of Palojax, opened its mouth and let out a long, low growl that sounded as if an enormous geyser had just erupted. "What brings you to the Below?" the frightclops asked with an ear-rumbling roar. "Do you wish to tell tales of my glory?"

The fiery cobra head twisted in front of the frightclops. "Let me eat them," the cobra begged, the words slithering from its lips. "I have not tasted flesh from the Above in so long."

The bear head roared, exposing its bloody teeth.

"Patience," the frightclops said to the other heads. "You may desire food, but I welcome a bit of conversation before I dine."

"We need you to return to the surface," Wily said. "Neccanite golems are marching on the land again."

"Tell me more about your misery," the frightclops said. "I find it amusing."

Wily was still trying to find Valor. Looking around, he spotted something in the cracks of the earth, just beyond the heads of Palojax: a pair of hands moving along the edge of a crack, slowly making their way to the side of the beast. Yes, it was Valor! She'd found a way to sneak up on the lair beast. They just needed to hold the creature's attention a little bit longer. If Valor could get on the back of Palojax, Wily was certain she'd be able to quell it, just like she had the manticorn.

"If we don't gain your assistance, all of the Above will be squashed underfoot by the mighty golems," Wily said, emphasizing the miserable details. "Homes will be shattered to splinters of wood. People will run screaming in terror."

"Go on," the frightclops said with delight. "I have not heard a story for so long."

Wily could see Valor was making progress toward Palojax but would need more time.

"And the cavern mages," Wily offered, "will enslave every elf, gwarf, and squatling. Even the great beasts of the forest and sea will have nowhere to hide."

"That may be worth seeing," the frightclops roared.

"I'm hungry *now*," hissed the cobra head. It spat a stream of acid at Wily and Roveeka. Pryvyd jumped forward and blocked the attack with his shield.

The bear head growled with anger.

"I can't stop my other two heads from devouring you," the frightclops said. "It's time for them to eat."

"Let me tell you one last horrible thing," Wily implored.

He could see that Valor was climbing out from the crack in the ground. She only needed a slightly longer distraction and she would be able to leap onto the beast's back.

"No," the frightclops said as the beast's body began to move. "It's feeding time."

The cobra head lunged for Odette. She tossed one of the yellow mushrooms in the palm of her hand at the face of the giant snake. When the mushrooms exploded, they created a noxious mist that would knock a smaller creature unconscious within a second, but the snake swallowed the mushroom whole . . . and nothing at all happened.

"You think that a noxshroom will do anything to us?" the frightclops asked. "There is nothing that grows on the back of your moss golem that will harm me. I am a battle you cannot win."

Roveeka threw Mum with all the force and precision that had made her a famous knife-wielder in Carrion Tomb. The lair beast lazily flapped one of its batwings, causing a *whoosh* of air to blast forth, and the sharp blade was sent flying back to Roveeka like a boomerang.

"Why do you even bother?" the frightclops asked as the bear head let out another fierce howl. "You are like fleas on the back of a gristle hound."

Wily could see Valor was now on her feet. She was half limping, half running as fast as she could on her injured leg. She gritted her teeth, fighting through the pain, and made a running leap for the rear of the lair beast. Palojax didn't spot her until it was too late. The lair beast's spiked tail tried to swat her away like a fly but it struck nothing but air.

Wily watched Valor scurry up the back of the beast. Palojax's tentacles tried to grab her but she was too swift. She was going to make it.

"Get off me," the frightclops growled.

Valor reached the base of the three necks and stretched her arms to press down on the pressure points on both sides of Palojax's spine. But she seemed to be struggling. "I can't reach both spots at the same time," Valor shouted. "The beast's spine is too big. Wily, I need your help!"

Wily froze. *I can't do it,* he thought. He felt a wave of pressure roll over him like a large lava wave.

He was surprised when he felt a hand squeeze his.

It was Roveeka. "You won't hit any target if you don't throw the knife," she said.

Wily nodded. He had to try. He spun to Moshul and grabbed a purple mushroom off his leg, then handed it to Roveeka.

"You know what to do," he said to her.

Wily started to run for Palojax as Roveeka threw the mushroom at the ground. It exploded in a giant cloud of smoke.

Wily had to time this perfectly. As soon as the smoke surrounded him, he came to a sudden stop. He felt a rush of air as the cobra head snapped down at the exact spot he would have been if he'd continued running. He bolted for the back of the snake head and jumped on.

The batwings blew away the mushroom smoke as the cobra head lifted into the air with Wily on top.

"Did you catch him?" the frightclops asked.

"He's on my head," the cobra hissed.

But he wouldn't be for long. Wily sat down on the cobra head and went speeding down its curved back like it was a giant twisting slide. He landed with a thump next to Valor.

"Pressure points *now,*" Valor said.

Wily jabbed his fingers directly into one spot where the heads joined together while, across the beast's wide spine, Valor jabbed the other. Wily felt his fingers shove into the tough, leathery skin of the creature.

Palojax began to writhe. Every tentacle flailed in anger. The cobra head tried to twist backward to snatch the two humans.

"Harder," Valor said. "There are a lot of animals and wall-dwellers counting on us."

"Now you want to save the wall-dwellers too?" Wily asked as he dug his fingers in.

"I might have misjudged your people," Valor said with a faint smile. "Push even harder."

"I'll try my best," Wily said, giving it his all.

"That's all you can do. You've already done more than anyone could have expected." Valor's words were full of sincerity. "I believe in you."

Wily looked over at his friends to see them staring back at him proudly. *They believe in me too.* He continued to press down on Palojax's spine with all his might. *And I believe in me.* Suddenly, he felt a weight lift from his shoulders. He was filled with a confidence that he hadn't felt since his days in Carrion Tomb. All the pressure he had been putting on himself was gone.

At that same instant, Wily felt the great lair beast relax beneath him. As Valor and Wily continued to press down, Palojax's whole body seemed to calm.

"Command it," Valor said. "Firmly and with confidence."

"You will return to the surface once more," Wily said, "and help us defeat the army of stone that threatens the land."

"I will help," the frightclops said.

Suddenly, Wily felt as giant as the lair beast.

"Have your companions climb on my back," the frightclops said.

"We will not bite," the cobra head said.

"Good job," Valor said. She gave Wily a big hug.

Palojax lowered its body onto the ground. One after the other, Wily's friends climbed up the batwing Palojax had extended like a ramp. Only Moshul seemed hesitant to pass the tentacles.

"Get up there, you big bundle of daisies," Pryvyd said to the moss golem.

Once all were onboard, Palojax flapped its giant batwings. They took off from the surface of the upside-down sun and started flying straight up toward a hole in the roof of the Below. Palojax raced past the upside-down hanging trees toward a wide tunnel in the ceiling.

As they blasted into it, everything went dark, but moments later the bear head let out a burst of glowing frost from its lips.

Wily peeked through the gap between the heads of the lair beast as it sped higher. They were heading for what appeared to be a wall of stone.

"We're going to crash!"

"Don't worry," the frightclops said. "It's only ten feet of solid rock. Brace yourselves."

Wily held on for dear life and squeezed his eyes shut. Palojax plowed straight into the wall, demolishing the barrier. Huge chunks of rock exploded outward. When Wily dared open his eyes again, he was surrounded by blue sky.

"It's even more beautiful than I remember," Palojax said.

# THE THREE-HORNED HELMET

Looking down from Palojax's back, Wily could see they'd blasted out of the side of Cloudscrape Peak many miles to the north of the royal palace. From this height, everything below looked like the magical map in the palace's reading room.

"To the south," Wily called out to Palojax. "Past the lake and—"

"I remember where the palace is," the frightclops said. "I was there when it was first being built."

Palojax gave a mighty flap of its large batwings, propelling them even higher into the sky. Valor sat next to Wily, peering over the side of the beast just like Wily. Below they could see a trail of ravaged forests and towns, most surely the work of the stone golem army. Wily hoped dearly they weren't already too late.

Pryvyd relaxed as the wind blew across his face.

Righteous, on the other hand, was holding its sword aloft, careful to brandish it every time the fiery cobra looked back at them. Moshul sat in the middle of the great beast's back, making sure he was as far away from the beast's slimy tentacles as possible.

Roveeka climbed up onto Moshul's back and reached her hands upward. "I can almost touch the cloubs," she said.

"They're called clouds," Odette corrected.

"I don't care what they're called," Roveeka said. "I want to catch one and use it as my pillow."

"You go right ahead," Odette said.

Roveeka kept reaching into the clouds and tried to snag the moist air, with little success. "I wish all the hobgoblets of Undertown were here to see this," Roveeka said as she waved her arms.

Before long, the great lair beast was flying over the mountains north of the royal palace. Moving closer to their destination, they passed over the prisonaut.

"Wait," Wily called out to Palojax. "Stop there."

"What are you doing?" Odette asked.

"My father's involved in Stalag's plan," Wily said. "I need to know how."

As Palojax swooped out of the clouds and descended in a majestic spiral toward the prisonaut, Wily could see the women and men patrolling the high walls take cover behind their shields in fear. The lair beast landed with enough force to make all of Trumpet Pass tremble. Wily quickly hustled to the top of the frightclops's head and waved his arms to signal the guards.

"Prince Wily?" a soldier called out, puzzled.

"I need to know how and when my father escaped from the prisonaut and if he left any clues behind," Wily called out. "Did he use the screwdriver?"

The soldier looked puzzled.

"Escaped? You must be mistaken. He's in his cell downstairs."

"I think you better check again," Wily said.

The soldier ran for the stairs in a panic. It took only a short moment before she was running back to the wall.

"Prince Wily," she called out, "Kestrel Gromanov is still in his cell."

"Are you sure it's not a mechanical man he built?" Wily asked.

"I touched him with my own hand," the soldier said. "There is no question."

"I don't understand," Wily said. "The acorns showed a three-horned helmet just like the one my father wore when he was the Infernal King."

"She also told us to hide in the mud when danger came," Valor said. "Maybe she never thought we would actually get the lair beast to join us. Nobody can see the future in its entirety."

"But the mural at Halberd Keep showed the planned attack on the royal palace," Wily continued. "The Infernal King was part of that plan."

"What does a wall know?" Roveeka said.

"The only walls I'm concerned with right now," Odette said, "are the palace's. We need to get there before the stone golems turn them to rubble."

Wily nodded. "Palojax," he shouted, "take us to the palace!"

The guards of the prisonaut took cover as the lair beast launched into the air once more. Wily's mind was racing as Palojax flew to the outer walls of the royal palace. There were still so many questions. If the Oracle of Oak wasn't mistaken, what did the three-horned helmet in her acorns mean? Could his father have been plotting something from within the prisonaut? And had Stalag and the cavern mages found the neccanite they'd been looking for? Wily just hoped that his mother, the Knights of the Golden Sun, and the just people of Panthasos had been able to hold off the golems.

As they approached the royal palace, Wily was puzzled to see only a small group of soldiers standing in a line beside the drawbridge.

"Where are all the other soldiers?" Wily shouted before Palojax had even landed.

"They already left with your mother," the soldier called back, "to face Stalag's army of stone golems, cavern mages, and bone soldiers on the dry plains beyond Trumpet Pass. By now, the battle may have already begun."

Palojax didn't need to be told where to go next. It

tilted its wings and soared for the Parchlands. Wily's heart was beating as strongly as the wings of the great lair beast as they came through the mountains.

"Look down there," Odette shouted, pointing into the distance.

On the ground, two hundred stone golems were marching across the field toward Trumpet Pass, their heads nearly knocking into the aqueducts that zigzagged above them. Some of the golems were armed with clubs, others with swords, and still others with nothing but their fists. They were joined by hooded cavern mages, hobgoblets, bone soldiers, and oglodytes. Girthbellow hovered beside his troop of slither trolls. Leading them all on the back of a giant scorpion was none other than Stalag himself.

Facing them was an army of humans, elves, gwarfs, and squatlings, forming a line across the dried fields, blocking the way to the royal palace. Wily could see his mother on the back of her horse, dressed in her Scarf outfit, parading in front of the line. The forces of good looked insignificant in the face of the coming threat, but they let out a loud cheer when they saw Palojax diving out of the sky and elegantly landing in the dry grass between the opposing forces. Wily realized just how crucial the lair beast was going to be in the coming battle.

Stalag raised a bony hand up in the air, signaling his army of golems to stand in place. The oglodytes and boarcus seemed ready to flee in panic. Agorop and Sceely sat on their own scorpions, looking terrified.

"I see that you have succeeded in your task," Stalag shouted. Strangely, he didn't seem to be particularly afraid of the legendary lair beast.

"I won't let you take the palace," Wily shouted back, "or any of Panthasos. Palojax defeated the golems before; he'll be able to do it again."

Palojax extended a wing, allowing the tip to lay flat on the ground. Wily and his companions slid down it and stepped onto the dry earth of the Parchlands.

"He looks old and tired," Stalag said with a ghoulish smile. "I don't think he's ready for this day." He addressed Palojax directly. "Go back to the Below and hide away once more. This is not your fight."

The bear head of the lair beast let out a roar. Then the frightclops spoke. "You have made a foolish choice, mage."

"Alabaster, Quartz," Stalag called to the two stone golems that had thrown Moshul from the mountain. "Show them what you can do."

The two stone golems ran for Palojax with clubs ready for pounding. The lair beast swung its spiked tail in a wide arc. The ball at the end hit the quartz-fingered golem in the chest, sending chips of stone flying as he was knocked off his feet. The alabaster-bearded golem lifted his club but never even got a chance to swing;

Palojax's fiery cobra fangs clamped down on his arm and ripped it clean off.

"My arm!" the mighty golem cried out.

"You've underestimated me for the last time," Wily told Stalag. "Call back your golems now. And leave Panthasos forever."

"I've never underestimated you, son," Stalag said. "I knew what you were planning. The oracle told me long ago. That's why I needed you to get me the enchanted compass. I knew there would be no other way to find the neccanite."

Wily looked out at the golems standing beneath the aqueducts. All were white and gray, not a black one among them. "I don't see any neccanite golems," he said.

"That's because I built only one," Stalag said.

"You're about to be grovblundered!" Agorop shouted gleefully.

"Yes," Girthbellow shouted. "There will be no cherry tomatoes to save your life this time."

"What are you talking about?" Wily asked, dread rising within him.

"May I present," Stalag shouted, "the Infernal Golem."

The mage raised his bony fingers into the air and fired a crackling bolt of darkness into the sky. The earth trembled with such force that Wily had to spread his legs and arms to balance himself.

Then, out from between the high mountains, an

enormous figure emerged—a golem of neccanite so big it made all the other golems look like children. The golem's head had been carved into a giant helmet with three horns—exactly like the helmet of the Infernal King.

"I thought this would be a fitting means of your destruction." Stalag's evil grin made Wily's heart sink.

This was the threat the oracle's acorns had shown.

The Infernal Golem marched across the earth, shaking it to its core, stepping over the aqueducts as if they were just sticks that had been tossed on the ground.

"Boy, do you really want to rule all of Panthasos?" Stalag taunted Wily. "It's a very big job for someone as young and sheltered as yourself. You'll only fail."

Palojax's three heads let out a mighty yell in unison, and the lair beast took to the sky. It flapped toward the sun before diving, heading straight for the Infernal Golem. But before Palojax could strike, the Infernal Golem grabbed the lair beast by the tail, plucking it out of the air. Then, with what seemed like no effort at all, he tossed the mighty lair beast back into the sky with such force that Palojax disappeared into the clouds.

The lair beast wasn't ready to surrender, though; it came shooting back out of the clouds and struck the Infernal Golem in the chest. Yet the great neccanite giant didn't even seem to notice the beast's attack. The golem lifted up the lair beast and threw it back toward Wily and his companions. They dodged out of the way as Palojax struck the earth, making a crater from the impact. Once the dust settled, Wily could see that the lair beast looked terrified, fearful expressions on all three of its faces.

"You have nothing to do now but run and hide," Stalag said with a laugh that made Wily's arm hair bristle.

"The oracle told us to sink into the mud," Pryvyd said, dropping his shield to his side. "I'm afraid to say that right now, it doesn't seem like such a terrible choice."

"I'm not ready to give up," Wily said. "And I'm never going to hide away below the surface of the earth ever again." He turned to the army standing in wait and called out to them in the loudest voice he could muster. "If we all stand tall together, we may defeat Stalag and we may not. But at least we'll have tried."

Lumina nodded from the back of her horse. All the humans, elves, and squatlings raised their weapons in support. Righteous raised its sword so high the disembodied arm was practically soaring skyward.

Wily called out to the recovering Palojax, "You battle the stone golems. We'll take on the oglodytes and hobgoblets and cavern mages."

"And what will we do against the Infernal Golem?" Pryvyd asked.

"Fight it together as one," Wily said. "With you all by my side, I feel like anything's possible."

"We wouldn't want to be anywhere else," Roveeka said.

"Actually, I'd prefer to be picnicking in a peaceful glen," Valor said.

"That's a good point," Roveeka said. "I would like that better too. Especially if we had some mushroom skewers."

"But if we are to be standing in the face of insurmountable odds," Valor said, "I want to do it at your side."

"For Panthasos," Pryvyd called as Righteous pointed its sword ahead.

The army of humans, elves, and squatlings charged toward the mass of bone soldiers that composed Stalag's front line. As they moved closer to the enemy, Wily suddenly realized just how greatly outnumbered they were. There were three walking skeletons for every one of their warriors.

"There aren't enough of us," Wily said.

"We need a whole extra army," Odette said.

"Good idea," Roveeka said from high on Moshul's shoulders. She cupped her hands and shouted at the top of her lungs. "I am the Grand Slouch. And I need your help. Stand by my side."

Cavern mages, slither trolls, and bone soldiers looked up at the tiny hobgoblet with amusement.

"Your rambles don't scare us," Girthbellow said. "Go back to the Below, little girl. You are not—"

A club knocked Girthbellow out of the air. The cavern mage looked around to find a dozen formerly loyal hobgoblets tackling him.

All the other cavern mages, slither trolls, and bone soldiers were swarmed from behind by the rest of the hobgoblets. "Grand Slouch! Grand Slouch! Grand Slouch!" they cheered.

"You wanted an extra army," Roveeka said as she slipped down from Moshul's back. "You got one."

"A mere distraction," Stalag said from his scorpion mount. "Golems!"

Before they could even move, Moshul went racing toward the alabaster-bearded golem. And despite being only made of mud and moss, Moshul seemed to possess a strength twice that of the stone golem. He knocked the bearded golem back against one of the support columns of an aqueduct. It caused a small crack above, raining a shower of water down on the golem's head. The waters spilled down his body like a waterfall.

Wily, along with the army of squatling, humans, elves—and now hobgoblets switching sides—went running past the fallen golem to face Stalag's minions in hand-to-hand combat. As Wily passed he could see that the bearded golem was struggling to get back on his feet, but it was caught in the mud forming below the leaking aqueduct. Wily's lighter weight allowed him to avoid the mire.

"Watch your steps," Wily called out to his army. "You don't want to sink into this mud."

And then he came to a dead stop. Wily looked at his

feet, ankle-deep in mud. He reached down and grabbed a thick clump of it in his fingers.

"Change of plans!" Wily shouted at the top of his lungs.

Odette looked at Wily. "We're going to have a mud fight?" she asked.

"The oracle wasn't telling *us* to sink into the mud," Wily said. "She was giving us a clue on how to defeat the Infernal Golem. We need to make *him* sink into the mud."

"Whoa!" Roveeka exclaimed. "Those acorns sure do know a lot."

"This time around," Wily said, "I don't need to make a new invention. I just need to break one I already made." He turned to Palojax and shouted, "I want you to break the aqueducts."

Stalag had seen the bearded golem struggling to free himself from the mud, and when he heard Wily's order to Palojax, he immediately understood what his former trapsmith was trying to do.

"Stop him!" Stalag called out to Agorop and Sceely. "Don't let him get on the back of that lair beast!"

Agorop and Sceely urged their scorpions forward, racing to beat Wily to Palojax. Sceely came charging up on her mount as Wily ran up the lair beast's wing. The lair beast took flight once more with Wily on its back, but Sceely jumped onto Palojax's side.

"Really?" Wily called back to her. "Are we doing this again?"

"Guess so," Sceely said as she came charging for Wily with her trident in hand.

She had made it halfway across the back of the lair beast when the fiery cobra head turned and snapped at the oglodyte. Sceely jumped back just in time to save herself from being eaten, but in the process she slipped and ended up dangling from one of the beast's squirming tentacles. She wasn't able to hold on, slipped again, and went tumbling down—right into the flowing water of an aqueduct.

Wily pointed to a spot in the long tube of rushing water. "Over there!" he shouted.

Palojax dove down and swung its tail at the elevated stream. The aqueduct exploded, sending water gushing to the ground. Palojax continued onward to the next stretch of aqueduct that descended from the hills. Wily gripped on tightly as the lair beast blasted through the side of the stone supports, sending another river gushing down onto the parched earth.

Wily looked back over his shoulder and saw the broken aqueducts were dumping huge amounts of water onto the ground. A pair of stone golems stood in the middle of the rapidly forming lake of mud and attempted to escape, but with each step they sank deeper into the wet earth.

Palojax struck three more aqueducts in rapid succession. It was as if multiple rivers were now suddenly converging into one area of the plains. The pools of water formed by the flowing lakes began to overlap.

The Infernal Golem was standing in the center of all the broken aqueducts and trying to grab the lair beast from the sky, but Wily and Palojax were too high to be caught. The Infernal Golem took three mighty steps before the ground gave out beneath it. A giant sinkhole formed, swallowing the Infernal Golem up to its waist. The mighty golem tried to pull itself out, but its efforts only made it sink deeper into the mire.

As Wily and the lair beast flew by, he could hear Stalag screaming at the Infernal Golem. "Get out of there!"

The Infernal Golem tried to grab a nearby aqueduct column to pull itself free. Instead, it ripped the column straight out of the ground. Just then, the sinkhole collapsed in on itself, pulling the Infernal Golem into the abyss.

Wily commanded Palojax to fly over the place where the earth had opened up. He could see that the sinkhole dropped away into nothingness, but he thought he could discern the faintest of glows at the bottom and wondered if the Infernal Golem had dropped all the way to the Below.

Wily signaled Palojax to touch down on the hillside overlooking the battlefield. As the hundreds of stone golems struggled to move in the mud, the cavern mages found themselves in rapidly rising water and tried to escape by swimming. Unfortunately, the strong current made it difficult for them to stay afloat. Elves and squatlings paddled out on wooden shields to rescue them from drowning. The hobgoblets tied the captured up under the command of Roveeka.

The bone soldiers fared even less well. The rushing water had by now formed a whirlpool and quickly sucked the skeletons into the abyss as well. Only the oglodytes, who were excellent swimmers, managed to make it to shore by themselves—where they were quickly captured.

Wily saw Stalag standing on the back of his giant scorpion, which was floating like a log in the current.

"You're trapped," Wily called out. "Surrender and no harm will come to you."

"It would have been easier if you had just let me take the throne," Stalag said as he started to mumble a series of chants.

Wily had heard this spell twice before, once in Stalag's study when the cavern mage cast it on a snap-lizard and another time on Agorop in the Floating City. Something began to grow in Stalag's hands. As it expanded in size, Wily realized it was a cave cricket.

"Catch him before he gets away," Wily called out to Palojax.

The cricket was now so huge that Stalag had to wrap his arms around it. As the lair beast flew at Stalag, the cricket leaped into the sky. Palojax dove for them, but the cricket was too quick for the three-headed beast.

Wily watched as Stalag bounded away on the cricket. As the cavern mage disappeared into the hills, he hoped dearly that he would never see his pale frame and quivering eyes ever again. But somehow he knew that he hadn't seen the last of the mage of Carrion Tomb. He couldn't believe that he'd let Stalag get away again.

Yet his disappointment was short-lived. When he turned back to his army, he saw a sea of smiling faces. "To the King of the Above," the knights cheered as they lifted Wily into the air.

"And the Queen of the Below," the elves yelled as the lifted Roveeka into the air beside Wily.

"Grand Slouch. Grand Slouch," the hobgoblets chanted as they thrust their fists into the air.

"This is going to go straight to the heads of those two," Odette said to Valor as she gestured to Wily and Roveeka.

"Probably," Valor answered. "But I think they deserve it."

# 21

# FLIP OF THE COIN

"You can do better than that, slowpoke!" Valor called out as she ran through the apple orchard, her injured leg already healed.

Wily was sprinting as fast as he could to catch up—but over the last week, he had lost every race. Yet he didn't mind at all.

"I'm coming for you," Wily shouted.

The finish line was just a hundred paces ahead. As he ran, he thought about all that had happened since Stalag's defeat.

The ferocious Palojax had returned to its peaceful and quiet home in the Below, but not before a huge celebration was held in its honor.

Locksage engineers were busy repairing and rebuilding the aqueducts. The remaining stone golems were given new masters and had now been tasked with repairing the destruction they had caused. The prisonaut that had until recently only housed Wily's father, Kestrel Gromanov, was now filled with cavern mages, oglodytes, and boarcus.

Wily's feet seemed to fly above the ground. Yet Valor easily crossed the finish line before him. She wiped a single droplet of sweat from her forehead as she took a swig of water from a mug.

"I'll beat you next time," Wily said, huffing, his face running with sweat.

"Not unless you invent something to make you run faster," Valor said with a good-natured grin.

"That's an interesting idea," Wily said.

"Of course, that would also be cheating."

"Says who?" Wily asked.

"Basic Roamabout regulations state you have to be barefoot for a footrace. When my tribe comes to visit the palace next week, you're going to have to take off your shoes for the round-the-garden sprint."

"Valor," a voice called from behind them.

Wily and Valor both turned to see Lumina standing there.

"Do you think we could talk?" she asked gently. "I know it's been a while, but I'd really like to get to know you."

Valor was silent for a moment, and then answered quietly, "Okay, Auntie."

The two moved into the trees and found a spot to sit.

Wily headed back for the drawbridge of the palace. Before he stepped onto the bridge, he glanced back over his shoulder. There, in the orchard, Valor and Lumina were hugging. It was a very good start.

Wily crossed the drawbridge and moved into the palace's rose garden, where he found Moshul constructing a stone bench. The seat was made of gray marble, but that wasn't the interesting part of the bench. The two legs were made with the heads of the alabaster-bearded and the quartz-fingered stone golems. Moshul had insisted that these two golems didn't get the honor of serving new masters.

"This is humiliating," the bearded golem complained. "We are mighty stone golems."

"You're right," Wily said as he approached. "And you deserve far worse."

Moshul happily took a seat on the bench. He kicked up his legs as the heads continued to complain.

"You need to put us back on our bodies," the head of the quartz-fingered golem said.

"At once," the other head said.

Moshul shook his head "no." Then the moss golem closed his eyes. As he did, flower blossoms opened up all down his body.

Wily moved on into the palace atrium. The room that had previously been filled with gifts from all over

Panthasos was now stuffed to the brim with even more thank-you presents from towns that had been attacked by the stone golems. Pryvyd and Odette were helping to arrange the gifts on shelves and tables.

"If we keep on saving the land," Pryvyd said, "we might have to build a museum for all these."

"Wily," Odette said, "we were just about to play a game of honey beetle with some of the guards. You want to play?"

"I didn't say I was playing," Pryvyd retorted. "I don't want honey all over my armor."

"It's gold," Odette said. "No one will notice if it gets a little messy."

Righteous was giving her words a big thumbs-up.

"Maybe later," Wily said. "I think I'm going to hit the library."

He walked up the steps into the quiet upper floors of the palace. They felt different from when he had left a fortnight earlier. The halls didn't feel stifling or tight any longer. Now they seemed comfortable and understanding. The whole palace felt like a place in which he could spend many happy years.

Wily walked into the library and was surprised to find Roveeka. She didn't know how to read and had yet to take an interest in learning. She stood before a glass display cabinet tucked in between two bookshelves.

"What are you looking at?" Wily asked.

"That coin," Roveeka said.

She pointed to a golden coin resting in a velvet case. The image of a sun was embossed on its surface.

"I think that might be the coin that was used for the Flip of Decision," she said. "It should never have been flipped at all."

"I agree," Wily said. "We should just tell the hobgoblets to move back to the surface. Who cares what happened hundreds of years ago?"

"You know that hobgoblets don't break their promises," Roveeka said. "They agreed to honor a fair wager and they got the cave instead of the sun. I just need to find a way to turn back time. Maybe if I bring the coin to the Oracle of Oak, she would know how to reverse time." Roveeka eyed the lock on the display cabinet. "You wouldn't happen to have the key, would you?"

"I don't," Wily said. "And I have no idea where to look for it. But I do have something just as good as a key."

Wily reached into his trapsmith belt and pulled out his replacement screwdriver. It took him only a minute to unscrew all the latches and hinges and completely remove the top of the display case.

Roveeka reached inside and pulled out the coin. Then she gave it a flip.

The coin landed in her palm sun up.

"And to think, humans could have just as easily flipped the other side up," Roveeka said.

She turned the coin around—only to see that the

back of the coin also held an image of the sun. Confused, she looked at Wily. They examined both sides.

There was no side with a cave on it.

"Maybe it's the wrong coin," Wily said.

"I don't think so," Roveeka said sadly. "I think the humans cheated. They knew they couldn't lose. That's why they chose to flip the coin."

Suddenly, Roveeka's frown turned into a big smile. "I did it!" she uttered in amazement. "I turned back time."

Wily looked at her as if she had lost her mind.

"The hobgoblets agreed to a fair wager," Roveeka explained. "But this wasn't a fair wager at all, so there's no promise for the hobgoblets to break if they come to the surface now."

"You are the Grandest Slouch of them all," Wily said.

"Looks like we're going to be having some new cooks in the kitchen soon," Roveeka said.

Wily felt mildly nauseated thinking of the black slime soup in Undertown. "As long as we keep some of the old ones too," he said.

"Naturally," Roveeka said. "But they're going to have some real competition now."

With a spring in her step, the hobgoblet hurried out of the library.

Wily turned to a big book sitting on the long oak table. He had helped save Panthasos again, but there was still a challenge that he hadn't succeeded in overcoming: learning to read. Odette kept telling him that if he continued studying, one day he would wake up and every-thing would just snap into place. But so far, it hadn't.

Wily sat down before the book and opened it. He took a deep breath, put his finger on the first word of the first line, and tried again.

# ACKNOWLEDGMENTS

Writing acknowledgments in a sequel is like attending a reunion. It's the opportunity to catch up with dear friends that you haven't seen in a while and tell them how much they mean to you.

So first I need to thank those who I have thanked before but whose contributions were no less (and perhaps even more) important this time around. Markus Hoffmann, my secret weapon in the world of words. The team at Imprint has done it again! Nicole Otto and John Morgan are editors that every writer would wish for; Wily and his companions' second adventure would be far less exciting without you. Iacopo Bruno created another stunning cover that brought Valor, Stalkeer, and Stalag to life in vivid color. Steve "Squiddoodle" Turner for the stunning endpapers that perfectly capture the wild inventions of Wily Snare. Natalie C. Sousa, your eye for design is second to none. Madison Furr and Mary Van Akin, who set up events in locations both near and far. And a huge thank-you to editor-in-chief Erin Stein for your continued passion and enthusiasm for a kid from the tomb.

I have had new friends accompany me on the journey to the Below who are in need of thanks. Where once I walked alone hand-in-hand with Trader Joe's Spiced Mangoes, they must now share my attention with the Trader Joe's Just Mango Slices. Spotify for hosting my Snared Playlist of fantasy inspiration, which is now public and available for your listening pleasure. And *Publishers Weekly* for the starred review that literally made me leap from my seat at a restaurant and start doing fist pumps.

I'd like to thank everyone who attended the book launch party at my house. It was a moment of true celebration and I was so happy to have old and new friends eat tacos and make slug slime in my company. A monster shout-out to Mrs. Craven's fifth grade class of '18 who was the very first group of students to read *Snared: Escape to the Above* aloud. To BookStar in Studio City for hosting my local bookstore signing and always placing my book facing outward. And to all the independent bookstore owners and employees across the globe I have spoken with and who have shared Wily with their young customers.

And after every good reunion . . . you return to your family. I would like to thank my mom and dad for being the East Coast marketing team, visiting bookstores and libraries with bookmarks and flyers. My daughter Olive for her careful inspection of *Snared: Lair of the Beast*'s cover and her massages when shoulders got tense. My daughter Penny who has learned to edit books while sitting on the couch in my office. (It is only a matter of time before you are writing a book of your own . . . or you start writing mine. There is most certainly a collaboration in the future.) And to my wife, Jane, with whom I have shared the last twenty years. Our marriage continues to be my greatest pleasure . . . even more than starred reviews.

# THE MONSOONODON

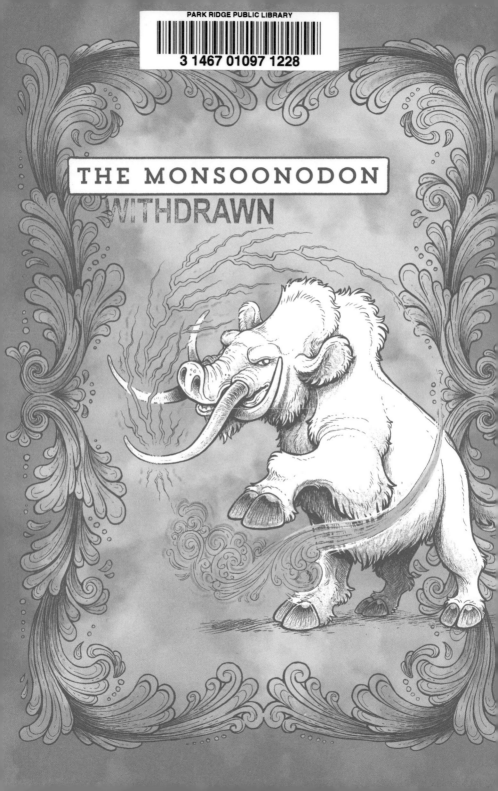